A SAFE HOUSE

A SAFE
HOUSE

—

STUART
WOODS

RANDOM HOUSE
LARGE PRINT

Copyright © 2022 by Stuart Woods

All rights reserved.
Published in the United States of America by Random House Large Print in association with G. P. Putnam's Sons, an imprint of Penguin Random House LLC, New York.

Cover illustration © Mike Heath

The Library of Congress has established a Cataloging-in-Publication record for this title.

ISBN: 978-0-593-55629-0

www.penguinrandomhouse.com/large-print-format-books

FIRST LARGE PRINT EDITION

Printed in the United States of America

1st Printing
This Large Print edition published in accord with the standards of the N.A.V.H.

A SAFE HOUSE

Stone Barrington and Dino Bacchetti were dining at their favorite restaurant, Patroon, on East Forty-Sixth Street in New York City, when simultaneously their chateaubriand for two was served as two gentlemen sat down at their table. Their names were Lance Cabot, director of the Central Intelligence Agency, and Henry Wilcox, his recently appointed deputy director for Operations.

"What a surprise!" Stone said. "And we were only expecting the steak."

"I apologize for interrupting your dinner," Wilcox said.

"Do you apologize for Lance, as well?"

"He does," Cabot said. "Don't let us slow you down."

Stone carved a slice of beef and put it into his mouth. "Well?" he said, after he had swallowed. "Would you like to see a menu?"

"We'll just order dessert," Lance said, raising a finger, which instantly summoned a waiter. "Two apple pies à la mode." The waiter vanished.

"Neither of you is watching your weight, then?" Stone asked.

The pies were set down before them and place settings produced. They dug in.

"We'll wait until you finish the pie before we ask what you're doing here," Stone said.

Neither of them spoke, but both kept eating. Lance finished first and held up the magic finger again. "Coffee for two," he said to the respondent waiter.

Stone and Dino kept eating.

The coffee arrived. "Now," Lance said.

"We're listening," Stone said, while still chewing his steak. "It may not seem so, but we are."

"There are two more gentlemen at this table than we require," Lance said.

"Are you telling my dinner guest and your deputy to go away?" Stone asked.

Lance said, "Since they both have my complete confidence, they may remain."

"Swell," Dino said.

"Stone," Lance said, "I am recalling you to active duty."

"You make it sound as if I'm in the Army Reserves."

"Pretty much the same thing," Lance said. "You are aware that you collect a monthly salary as my associate director."

"I seem to recall that," Stone said. "But the amount must be very small, since I can't remember how much it is."

"It's the principle of the thing," Lance responded.

"What is it you want, Lance?"

"I need you to provide a safe house for a person who shall remain unidentified, even with regard to gender."

"So, it's a woman?"

"Stop guessing. It's unbecoming. The person will be referred to in the editorial masculine."

"Okay, we'll pretend it's a man. What does he need? A bed for the night?"

"Several nights, perhaps many."

"At my house?"

"At your house in England."

"Will he make up his bed and be neat at all times?"

"I believe you employ staff to attend to those details."

"When may I expect him?"

"As soon as you can transport him there."

Stone blinked. "You want me to transport him

to my home in England and house him there, indefinitely?"

"For reasons I cannot explain to you, he may not be transported on an airline or government aircraft."

"So, you want me to fly him to England in my aircraft?"

"Yes, and accompany him—all in the strictest secrecy, of course."

"Of course. Why?"

"It's a secret."

"Oh, yes, you mentioned that."

"This is a person who has been of considerable value to the Agency. And if he survives, we trust he will be again."

"So his survival is in question?"

"There are powerful people who do not wish him well."

"Well, I would sure hate to be him," Stone said.

"Do not make light of this, Stone. It is too important."

"Important to whom?"

"Powerful people."

"I trust these are not the same powerful people who don't wish him well."

"There are all sorts of powerful people involved in this, Stone."

"And what will they do to me, if they should discover that I have transported this fellow to England and put him up in my house?"

"If they don't know that, they can't do any-thing to you, can they?"

"Don't make light of this, Lance."

"Stone, do you have any questions that are not annoying?"

"Two: Who pays for the airplane? And why me?"

"You may present me with a bill for the air-plane and fuel, at standard rates. As for why you, I have already reminded you that you are on salary."

"And when do you want me to do this?"

Lance gazed at his wristwatch. "How soon can you take off?"

"Lance," Stone said. "Not in the middle of a convivial dinner. Have the person at Teterboro at ten o'clock tomorrow morning. His driver should deliver him inside the Strategic Services hangar and put him aboard the airplane there. The crew will already be aboard. I and my guests will be along shortly after that."

"Guests?" Lance had turned pink. "There will be no guests aboard."

"You have already said that Dino has your complete confidence," Stone pointed out. "And I presume that confidence extends to his wife."

Lance worked his jaw a bit. "Oh, all right," he said, finally.

"I'll check our schedules," Dino said.

"Otherwise, who would I talk to during and

after the flight? It sounds as though I may not speak to the subject of this conversation."

"You should stay in England for at least a week," Lance said. "We can't have this looking like a simple delivery."

"I don't think that will be too much of a burden on my good nature," Stone said. "After all, it's my house. I love it and don't get there often enough."

"Me, either," Dino said.

Lance placed his palms on the table. "Well, that concludes our business, I think."

"Are we allowed to communicate with the person, and he with us?" Stone asked.

"Once you're clear of New York air space," Lance said, rising, and Wilcox with him. "The apple pie is on you," he said, and the two men left.

"Well," Stone said, "that was unexpected."

"Yeah, and you get a free trip to England and to your own house," Dino said.

"You coming?"

"Yeah, I can take some time. If Viv shows up tomorrow morning, she'll go, too. Otherwise . . ."

"She's off to Bangkok or somewhere."

"You know the drill."

Stone called Faith, his pilot, and gave her instructions for the morrow, then he and Dino ordered apple pie à la mode.

———

The following morning, Stone went down to his office and checked his desk for unresolved work. His secretary, Joan Robertson, walked in.

"I hear you're off to England," she said.

"I hear that, too," Stone replied. "Lance delivered the word personally last night at Patroon."

"Any idea how long?"

"At least a week. More, if I'm having fun."

"Oh, God, you always have fun."

"I forgot. You don't know about this trip. It's a big-time secret. I'm traveling, and you won't know where until you hear from me, and somehow, you won't. Take a message."

"Got it." She handed him a fat envelope. "Here's all the pounds sterling we had in the safe. I can't spend it here."

"Thank you." She started to return to her office. "Oh, I almost forgot. One of your guests has been delivered to the Strategic Services hangar and is safely—and secretly—aboard."

"Good to know."

"Safe trip."

"You betcha."

2

Fred delivered Stone and Dino to the Strategic Services hangar at Teterboro that morning at ten. Stone climbed the airstairs to the door while the ground crew dealt with his luggage. He found a large man with a lump under his arm standing guard over the door to the third compartment.

"The ground crew will need to get in there to stow the luggage aft," he said to the man, who thought about it, then opened the door a crack, said something, and closed it again. "The person is in the toilet," he said. "Your people may enter with the luggage." He opened the door and stood back.

"Thank you so much," Stone said, motioning the ground crew aft toward the luggage compartment. During the process, which took about a minute and a half, the guard remained, his back against the restroom door. When the luggage was stowed, he rapped twice on the toilet door, then stepped back into cabin two and closed the door behind him.

The airplane began to move, being towed by a tractor onto the ramp outside.

"We're about to start engines," Stone said. "Your work is done."

The man opened the door again, said a few words, then closed it and left the airplane.

Stone went to the cockpit door. "Start engines," he said, then took his seat opposite Dino. Viv was winging her way somewhere else.

"Any news on the cargo?" Dino asked.

"Not until we're out of New York air space," Stone reminded him.

"I forgot. The suspense is killing me."

"Yeah. Me, too," Stone replied.

Shortly, the airplane turned onto runway one and began to pick up speed. Seconds later, the pilot lifted off and the airplane climbed. At a couple thousand feet they got a vector and turned east.

"When does New York air space end?" Dino asked.

"I'm not sure. Let's call it Montauk."

"Okay with me."

As they passed Montauk Point, the eastern

tip of Long Island, the airplane was climbing through fifteen thousand feet, according to the display screen on the forward bulkhead. It continued to climb.

"Okay, that's it," Stone said. He unbuckled, got up, and walked to the third compartment door and knocked. There was a delay, then the door opened.

Stone knew her from somewhere. Model, he thought, but not recently. She wore pants and a silk blouse and had a sweater tied around her shoulders. "Yes?" she said.

"My name is Stone Barrington," he said. "I am your host. Would you like to join a friend and me up front? It's more comfortable there."

"Give me a minute or two," she replied, then closed the door.

Stone returned to his seat. "Okay," he said to Dino. "Female, fortyish, five-ten, beautifully dressed. I know her from somewhere, but I can't remember where. She'll join us shortly."

"That's it?"

"That's all I've got. You can grill her."

The woman came forward, her hair brushed and her makeup refreshed. Now she looked thirtyish. "Good morning," she said tentatively. "I'm Jenna Jacoby."

"Jenna, this is Dino Bacchetti."

"You're a policeman, aren't you?" she asked, shaking his hand.

"Dino is **the** policeman," Stone said. "New York City's police commissioner."

"Ah, yes," she said, taking a seat. "And, Mr. Barrington, who are you?"

"Please call me Stone."

"I'm sorry. I meant to ask, **what** are you?"

"I am an attorney, with the law firm of Woodman & Weld."

"That's good, isn't it?"

"We like to think so."

"Of course."

"You are a model, are you not?"

"**Was** a model, some years ago."

"How have you occupied yourself since then?"

She started to speak, then stopped. "I nearly said 'housewife,'" she said, "but that would not be accurate. My occupation, until this airplane passed Montauk Point, was the care and feeding of a United States senator."

Stone's brow furrowed. "I don't know of a Senator Jacoby."

"That's my maiden name, which I have re-adopted," she said. "His name was—is—Wallace Slade, Republican of Texas."

Stone tried not to make a face. "Oh, yes."

"I understand. Many people find the mention of his name distasteful," she said. "I am one of them."

"I see. Is that why you are . . . traveling with us today?"

"Not just the fact of being married to him. That's bad enough. But there have been two attempts on my life since I announced my intention to divorce him."

"What was the nature of those attempts?" Stone asked. "If you will pardon my asking."

"No pardon necessary. On the first occasion, I was driving my car, a convertible, and another car drew alongside of me and threw a considerable amount of a liquid into my car. I braked and got behind him, then I noticed that the seat fabric next to me was smoking and being eaten into. I got to a gas station, called a friend, and abandoned the car. The second time was when a man approached me in the parking lot of a shopping mall and fired a shot at me."

"What was the result of that?"

"I shot him back," she replied matter-of-factly. "One round, but I don't think I killed him."

"Did you call the police?"

"Yes. The first thing they asked me was why didn't I call them after the first attempt."

"What was your reply?"

"I told them the truth: I was too shaken to remember to do that."

"What period of time elapsed between the two attempts?"

"Ten days, two weeks."

"And were you in Washington at the time? Or in Texas?"

"I was at our ranch in Texas, where a phone call from my husband is enough to steer any investigation in whatever direction he wishes. The second attempt was outside Neiman Marcus, in Dallas."

"What was your husband's reaction when you told him about the attempts?"

"A failure to seem surprised."

Stone nodded. "Would you like some breakfast or lunch?"

"Lunch, please. Then I'll tell you the rest."

3

They were served a large lobster salad and a bottle of a good Napa chardonnay, well chilled. She showed no tendency to talk while they were eating.

"Ms. Jacoby?" Stone said, when they were having coffee.

"Jenna, please."

"Jenna, you're clearly an intelligent person, so I'm not going to treat you as a dumb housewife."

"Thank you."

"I'm going to ask you some questions, and I would be grateful for honest and detailed answers. If you can give me that, then you will be safer in my care. And I will know what is going on here, which, at this moment, I don't understand."

"What don't you understand?" she asked.

"I don't know why, instead of being treated as a domestic beef, one followed twice by attempted maiming or murder, the chief federal intelligence agency has involved itself in this affair, which would normally be investigated by the police, the sheriff, or the Texas Rangers."

"I believe I told you that my husband has the power to make those agencies go away and return to giving speeding tickets, or whatever they normally do."

"That part I understand," Stone said. "What I don't understand is why the CIA is interested in you and your domestic circumstances and why it's a good idea to hide you."

"Oh," she said. "That."

"Yes, that."

She gazed out a window. "I was recently interviewed, at some length, by investigators from the Senate Select Committee on Intelligence and the Senate Committee on Foreign Relations."

"What, as briefly as you can tell me, did they want to know?"

"They wanted to know if a United States senator of my acquaintance is involved with at least one foreign intelligence service, that of the Russian government, to the extent of being a spy for them against his own country."

Stone blinked and tried to digest that.

"I know," she said. "I was dumbfounded, too, when that came up during my interview."

"How did you respond?"

"With an affirmative reply."

"How did you come to the attention of these committee investigators?"

"When I suspected my husband of such activity, I called the only person I knew who was involved with American intelligence."

"Lance Cabot," Stone said tonelessly.

She furrowed her brow. "And how did you come to know that?" she said. She looked around, as if for a way to escape an airplane at forty thousand feet.

"It was Lance who interrupted my dinner with Dino last evening and asked me to provide you with a safe house."

"A 'safe house'?"

"It is a term used by intelligence agencies to describe a place where a person of interest can be sequestered from contact with others, in order to assure that person's safety."

"Is that where we are going now?" she asked.

"Lance didn't brief you on this?"

"I haven't spoken to Lance since yesterday, when I first called him."

"I see."

She looked out the window. "We appear to be flying across the Atlantic Ocean," she said.

"Let me explain, to the extent that I can: Lance

wants you in a safe place, and he knows that I have a house in the countryside of southern England, which has its own landing field, one dating back to World War II. He knows that I am acquainted with his British counterpart, Dame Felicity Devonshire, who is the head of Britain's foreign intelligence service and my neighbor there, and who will be assisting us in ways not yet known to me. He doubts that your husband or his Russian colleagues will be able to figure out where you have gone. So Lance has had you smuggled aboard my airplane, not even mentioning your gender, let alone your name or that of your husband."

"How large a house?" Jenna asked him.

"Large, by American standards; cozy, by the measure of the British aristocracy. You will be quite comfortable, I assure you."

She looked out the window again and thought about it. "Do you have horses?" she asked.

"Yes."

"For riding?"

"Yes, not for plowing."

Jenna smiled for the first time. "Then I am sure I will be quite comfortable," she said. "How long will I be there?"

"I think that will be up to Lance Cabot," Stone said, "but I'm sure he will consult with you on that matter. Let me give you the lay of the land."

"Please."

"The house is Georgian, but has, in recent years, been thoroughly renovated. So it has, as the Brits like to put it, 'all mod cons.'"

"All modern conveniences?"

"Flush toilets and everything."

"Tell me about this landing field."

"The British intelligence services requisitioned the property at the onset of the war—as they did of many other country houses. And they constructed the airfield, which still does not appear on any aeronautical chart, as a facility for launching and retrieving intelligence officers to and from France. After the war, the property was returned to its original owners, who maintained the airfield up until the time I bought the place, and I have continued to do so. When we land, we will be met by customs officials from nearby Southampton Airport, who will admit us to the country. If I know Dame Felicity, their attention will be brief."

"Wallace would have Heathrow and Gatwick watched," Jenna said.

"Thus Lance's choice of me and my house."

"What is your relationship with Lance?"

"We chat from time to time," Stone replied. "Occasionally he makes an outrageous request of me, as I do of him. For his own convenience, he has appointed me an associate director of the CIA."

"What does that mean?" she asked.

"Absolutely nothing," Stone replied. "Except what Lance wants it to mean on some occasion or other."

"Well, Stone, it seems that I have fallen into what was once known as 'a pot of jam.'"

"I'll do my best to see that you remain there," Stone said.

S tone returned from the cockpit and sat down with Jenna and Dino. "We're about half an hour out," he said. "Dinner at the house will be awaiting our pleasure. You'll have time to freshen up and change, if you wish. But dinner will be informal, in the study instead of the dining room."

"Will anyone else be there?"

"If so, I haven't been informed of that," Stone replied. "But Dame Felicity will pop in, unannounced, at some point, and it could even be this evening."

"I imagine her as looking something like Agatha Christie," Jenna said.

Stone and Dino both laughed aloud.

"Not in the least," Stone said. "We've started

our descent, so you'd better buckle up." The descent was rapid, and there was only one turn required to line up with the runway.

"Is that your house?" Jenna asked, looking out a window when they were on short final.

"Yes," Stone replied.

"It's very handsome."

"Thank you."

The aircraft touched down gently and rolled to a stop in front of a large hangar, painted green to blend in with the landscape. A couple of vehicles sat on the tarmac before it. The plane's engines died, and an attendant opened the cabin door, with its airstairs.

"You'll meet Major Bugg now. He runs the estate and the house," Stone said.

The major greeted everyone and was introduced to Jenna without a mention of her name. "We're very happy to have you with us," he said to their guest. "My staff and I are at your disposal, if you need anything at all."

"Thank you, Major Bugg," she replied and got into the waiting Range Rover, the door of which was held open. They were driven to the house, while another vehicle followed with their luggage. Once there Major Bugg escorted Jenna to a large, beautifully furnished room, with a fireplace and some furniture at one end.

"Mr. Barrington requested that you be next

door to him, should you need his attention," he explained.

"That's kind of him," Jenna replied.

Stone appeared in the doorway. "Please join us in the study—downstairs, then on your right," he said. "Drinks in half an hour. But take as long as you wish."

————

Stone unpacked what little he had brought, since he already had a wardrobe in place. He showered, changed, and walked downstairs. He was only a little surprised to find Dame Felicity Devonshire sitting next to the fire with a martini on the small table beside her.

"Felicity!" Stone cried and bent to kiss her lightly on the lips.

"I'd want more than that, if I didn't have to redo my lipstick," she said. "So, where is your guest?"

"She's upstairs doing whatever it is that women do before coming downstairs."

"I've read her dossier," she said, "courtesy of Lance Cabot."

"That is a courtesy I was not extended," Stone said. "Lance went to extraordinary lengths to conceal her departure with us. I didn't even know she was a woman until we had left New York air space, but I managed to grill her fairly closely on the ride over."

"That husband of hers is a proper swine, isn't he?"

"We did not delve into that subject; perhaps tomorrow. It would be kind of you to leave her file with me, so that I have time to brush up on her story and situation before speaking to her again."

"Her story is fascinating," Dame Felicity said, "and her situation dire. I hope you can protect her."

"Dino is along to help, so I think between the two of us and the staff, we can manage that."

As if on cue, Dino entered, looking well-pressed and thirsty and greeted Felicity properly.

"I see your wife has escaped your clutches again," Felicity said.

"Yeah, she's sneaky that way; always off to someplace I can't pronounce—on business, she claims."

"Then she doesn't deserve you."

"She has never heard those words spoken, so don't you start."

Jenna now made her entrance, somewhat tentatively, as if she weren't sure she had found the right room.

Stone and Dino were on their feet. "Come in, Jenna," Stone said. "Dame Felicity, may I introduce Ms. Jenna Jacoby? Jenna, this is Dame Felicity Devonshire, of whom I have spoken."

The two women shook hands. "Just plain Felicity will do nicely," the elder one said.

"How do you do?" Jenna replied, offering a smile. Stone had not seen her smile until now, and he thought it becoming.

Stone tended bar for everyone, then took a seat next to Jenna. "Felicity has already read what the British call your **dossier**, so she won't have to grill you as I have."

"Thank heavens for that," she replied. "I'm not sure I have it in me to repeat all that."

"I trust Stone and his people have made you comfortable," Felicity said.

"Very much so," Jenna replied. "It's a lovely house, Stone, inside and out."

"I'm glad you think so," Stone replied.

"My dear," Felicity said. "If Stone becomes too demanding of your attentions, I'm just across the river, and I'll send my boatman for you. There you can find peace and solitude."

"Oh, I think I've already found peace here, and lately, I've had more solitude than I need. It's nice to have some company, though Dino has hardly spoken since I met him."

"I was stunned into silence," Dino said.

"Don't worry," Stone said, "by the time he starts his second Scotch, he'll be talking your ear off."

"I'll look forward to that," Jenna said.

They dined in the study on Dover sole, and

after dessert and cheese, Felicity said, "If you will all forgive me, I've had a long day. Stone, will you walk me to my cart?"

"Of course," he said, and he escorted her out of the house to a waiting golf cart, driven by a staffer.

Felicity kissed him properly, unmindful of her lipstick. "You be careful with that girl," she said. "I can tell that she's been deeply wounded. Let her heal a bit before you seduce her."

"I?" Stone asked in mock outrage.

"If you find yourself in need of a good fuck," she said, "come see me." Then the cart drove her away toward the river.

"I'll count on that," Stone called after her, then he returned to the house.

In deference to his guests, Stone went down to breakfast the following morning instead of having it in bed. She was ahead of him, and he joined her.

"Good morning, Jenna," he said. "I hope you slept well."

"Good morning, Stone. I did, thank you. My room was wonderfully silent, until the birds started up just before dawn."

"Yes, they do that."

"I pulled the pillow over my ears and went back to sleep."

"Good move."

"Do you think I might go riding this morning?"

"Of course. I'll go with you."

"That's not necessary."

"I'm sorry, but in the circumstances, I think it is."

"Do you think Wallace Slade would follow me over here?"

"You're in a better position to answer that," Stone said. "Would he?"

She thought about it for a moment. "Well, yes, he might very well send someone here looking for me."

"Then I hope you won't mind my company. Or one of the stable lads could go with you."

"I think I would prefer your company."

"Did you bring clothes?"

"Yes, except for a helmet."

"We will provide you with one."

"That would be very kind of you."

Stone's breakfast was delivered so he began to eat. "Can you tell me what happened recently to precipitate your disappearance from your usual haunts?"

"Two things, I think: one, Wallace somehow slipped up and allowed our divorce to become final, without trying to stop it."

"Had he been opposed to it earlier?"

"Vociferously," she said. "He had instructed his attorney to do everything he could to obstruct it."

"What changed his mind?"

"We had a court date for eleven AM, but my attorney appeared in the courtroom at nine, and before the judge could call his first case, my lawyer presented him with a final decree and a property agreement as well, and he offhandedly signed both. I guess Wallace had not gotten to him yet. So, voilà! I was a free woman and a fairly wealthy one, too. I was on the next flight to Washington, D.C., while Wallace was still at the ranch, sleeping one off."

"What was the other thing?"

"I met with committee investigators and was deposed, prior to my committee appearance."

"So Wallace knows you are on the record."

"He does. And the two events, on the same day, combined to make him apoplectic, I am reliably informed."

"By whom, may I ask?"

"My maid at the ranch house, who was fired during the same fit. I've seen to her welfare."

"And when are you expected to make your appearance before the committee?"

"In about two weeks; I'll receive a subpoena."

"In your absence from the ranch house, is there someone else who might keep you informed on events there?"

"Yes, Wallace's driver, whom he trusts implicitly, but who despises him."

"I would like to be informed of any news from the driver. What's his name?"

"Robert Parker."

"And the maid's name?"

"Rose Parker. She is the half sister of Robert, though Wallace doesn't know that."

"How will you communicate with these two people?"

"Robert provided me with a throwaway cell phone, which works here."

"Some historical questions, if I may?"

"Certainly."

"How did you meet Wallace?"

"At a cocktail party at my sister's home. I was working as an assistant to her husband, Democratic senator Harry Bruce, of New Mexico."

"What was your first impression of Wallace Slade?"

"What he wished it to be: charming, attentive, sometimes funny, but not always intentionally. Wallace is very good at wearing the appropriate face for an occasion."

"When were you married?"

"Eight months later."

"How long were you married?"

"Four years to the day."

"And how much of that time was happy?"

"About twenty minutes," she replied.

Stone laughed in spite of himself.

"Wallace became his real self almost immediately: loud, crass, short-tempered, and violent, among other endearing traits."

"How did his violence express itself?"

"Shoving, slapping, on a few occasions, punching."

"And how did you defend yourself."

"I fought back, as best I could, given his size and weight advantage. Once I bloodied his nose, which gave him two black eyes. He looked like a raccoon for about a week and couldn't go out without makeup."

Stone laughed again. "Did your response have any effect on Wallace?"

"He shouted more but hit me less."

"You're a brave woman."

"I have a temper, just as he does."

"How would you describe Wallace's feelings for you over the years?"

"He wanted a trophy wife, and I gave him that. I had been a sought-after model for years, and I had good clothes and wore the jewelry he gave me. He liked that. But his ardor cooled very quickly, which was all right with me, and he chose not to speak to me unless it was absolutely necessary. In the company of others, he behaved himself and paid me compliments. By now, he clearly despises me, and the feeling is, of course, mutual."

"Would you describe yourself as a woman scorned?"

"Scorned and scorning," she replied.

"Do you think Wallace wants you dead?"

"I firmly believe that he does. If I had not had

Lance's protection I would already be in my grave. Wallace knows that when my testimony becomes public, his career will be over, and he will very likely go to prison. Killing me would put an end to all of that, or he believes it would."

"Have you left any record of what you have told me?"

"Yes, the committee investigators recorded it visually and with audio. I allowed them to do that on the condition that I be given a copy of the tape."

"And were you?"

"Yes."

"And where does that tape reside, now?"

"With my personal attorney."

"Who is . . . ?"

"Herbert Fisher, of Woodman & Weld. We've met only once."

"Herb is my law partner and my friend. Why did Lance come to me, instead of Herb?"

"Does Herb have a country house?"

"A place in the Hamptons; he's very social out there."

"Then he would have been unsuitable as my guardian, would he not?"

"Probably so. It would have been hard for him to hide you."

"Does that bring you up to date?"

"I believe it does. Your mount awaits."

"Then let's not keep the poor animal waiting!"

6

Stone took Jenna on his usual route around his property, including a jump over a stone wall. Then they stopped and rested under a tree for a few minutes, while the horses munched grass.

"I am so happy to be here," Jenna said, looking around. "It's such a beautiful place."

"The place is happy to have you here," Stone said, "as is its proprietor."

"This is the first time in weeks that I have not felt fearful or unnerved."

"This place does that for me, too," Stone replied, "on the rare occasions that I have those feelings."

"I was impressed with Dame Felicity," she said.
"How so?"

"She's smart and funny."

"She was impressed with you, too."

"How could you tell?"

"She told me so. I should tell you that Felicity's tastes in romantic activity are broad and inclusive."

"Does that mean that she's likely to make a pass at me?"

"Nothing as gauche as that. If she's attracted to you, she'll tell you so, then extend an invitation."

"Does she know how to take no for an answer?"

"She does, and you shouldn't feel fretful around her. She's very discreet."

"But she likes both men and women?"

"Oh, yes. And sometimes together."

"I'm glad you told me."

"I didn't want you to be shocked."

"I'm not, though a little surprised."

"At what?"

"That she enjoys both genders. Does she have a preference?"

"No, she's the complete voluptuary. If you and I were in bed together, she'd think nothing of asking to join us."

"But she would ask."

"She would. She has perfect manners, at all times."

Jenna laughed, a pleasant sound, Stone thought. "Shall we ride on in?"

"Why not?"

He gave her a leg up, mounted himself, and they walked on. On their return, they let the horses to cool down before allowing a stable hand to water them.

Dino came out the back door of the house. "Good ride?"

"Oh, yes," Jenna replied.

"Stone, I got a call from Viv, who was at the Bangkok airport. She's going to fly into London and join us."

"Great!"

"Can a borrow a car to meet her at the airport? I've booked us into the Connaught, and we'll spend a couple of days up there before driving down."

"Of course, take the Bentley."

"You mean the car with the big sign on the bumper that says **Mug Me, I'm Rich**?"

"Oh, all right, take the Range Rover or the Porsche."

"I'll take the Range Rover. Viv doesn't travel light."

"As you wish. Will you stay for lunch?"

"I've already had something. I'll pack a bag and go now." He went back into the house.

"Well," Stone said, "I'm as sweaty as my horse. I think I'll have a shower before lunch."

"If Dino weren't here, I'd join you," she said playfully.

"He's leaving," Stone replied. As if in confirmation, Dino brushed past them in the hallway, carrying two suitcases. "See you in a few days," he said, and was gone out the back door.

"Feel free," Stone said, then went to his room.

He shaved and got into the shower. He had been there for a couple of minutes when the glass door opened, and Jenna stood there, statuesque and naked. "Knock, knock," she said, then stepped into the shower.

Stone received her in his arms, and it was a thrill.

———

They lay in bed a few minutes later, recovering, her damp head on his shoulder.

"Did I mention that I don't feel nervous or afraid anymore?"

"You did."

"I feel very relaxed, too. It must be the company."

"I'm glad you're relaxed," he said, and they got relaxed all over again.

———

After a good dinner they sat at the table over a glass of port and slices of Stilton, still relaxed.

The butler entered. "Excuse me, Mr. Barrington, but there's a call for you from the Connaught Hotel." He began clearing the dishes.

"That will be Dino," Stone said, going to a phone in the corner and lifting the receiver. "Hello?"

"Mr. Barrington, this is John Spence, the night manager at the Connaught."

"Good evening, Mr. Spence. I hope you're well."

"I am. And I apologize for the hour, but we had an inquiry at the desk a short time ago that I thought you should know about."

"Yes, go on."

"A large gentleman wearing a Stetson hat and western boots came to the desk and asked if you had checked in yet. I was not aware that you had made a reservation, so I checked and found that you had not. So I told him so, and that you were not expected. Commissioner Bacchetti is here, though."

"Did you tell him that?"

"No, just that you were not expected. He asked if he could have a room, and I told him we were fully booked. That is not strictly so, but I didn't like the feeling I was getting. He departed shortly after a look around the ground floor, apparently to see if you were in one of the bars."

"Mr. Spence, I don't think there's anything to worry about, but thank you for letting me know. I'd be grateful for another call, if he should return." They said good night and hung up. Stone returned to the table.

"Everything all right?"

"Let me describe someone to you: large gentle-man in a Stetson hat and western boots."

"That sounds like Wallace, except for the 'gentleman' part."

"Someone of that description inquired at the Connaught front desk to see if I were in residence or expected. They told him no on both counts and declined his request for a room, so it sounds as if he just arrived."

"Well, you asked if he would look for me here."

"I did, and you were right. I wonder if he knows about this house?"

"I don't know," she said.

"Well, I suppose we'd better sleep with the doors locked and a shotgun beside the bed."

"I suppose we'd better."

7

S tone called Dino at the Connaught.

"Yes?"

"It's Stone. Did Viv get in all right?"

"She did. She's in the shower now, washing off the Far East, she says."

"I just want to alert you to something."

"Alert away."

"Do you know what Jenna's ex-husband looks like?"

"Not really."

"Big guy. And he's wearing a Stetson and cowboy boots, never mind about being in London."

"Why do you mention that?"

"Because earlier tonight, he inquired at the Connaught's front desk about whether I was a guest or expected."

"He moves kind of fast, doesn't he?"

"He does. What surprises me is he's doing his own detective work himself, instead of farming it out."

"Does he know about the house in Hampshire?"

"Not as far as I know. But he knows enough about me to anticipate that I might be at the Connaught, as I would be, if I were in London."

"Don't blame you. That would bother me, too."

"If you get a sighting of him in your travels around the city, would you call me and track him as far as you can? I'd like to know where he's staying, since the Connaught denied him a room, and who he's seeing."

"Sure, that might even be more fun than watching Viv shop."

"Thanks, pal. Now I'd better get back and attend to things."

"Sure, you should." They hung up.

"Has Dino seen him?" Jenna asked.

"No, and that's a good thing. Does he spend a lot of time in London?"

"We were there twice since being married, once for Wimbledon and once for the Chelsea Flower Show, both my choices, not his. Wallace's tastes run to horse races that he has to rent suits for."

"Ascot and the Derby."

"Right. He was always restless in London and dismissive of people with upper-class accents."

"Everybody at Ascot and the Derby," Stone said.

"Right. He was there for the horses."

"Did he have any friends in London?"

"No, the people we knew that we ran into were always Americans, usually Texans, at Annabel's or ultra-expensive restaurants."

"Where did Wallace make his money?"

"Oil, but not very much of it. He liked to pretend that he had a lot more than he had, and after he was appointed to the Senate, he seemed to have more money to throw around."

"Bribes, no doubt."

"I wouldn't put it past him."

They finished their after-dinner port. "Ready for bed?"

"I've been ready since I got out of it the last time."

"Then let's do it," Stone said.

"Doing it was foremost in my mind."

———

They were awakened by Stone's cell phone, early the following morning.

"Hello?"

"It's Dino. We're at breakfast in the dining room, and guess who just walked in?"

"A man in a Stetson hat and cowboy boots?"

"Right, they took the hat away from him, and he didn't like that much."

"Are you game to find out where he goes after breakfast?"

"Sure. So's Viv. She loves this sort of stuff."

"Call me with a bulletin now and then."

"Will do." Dino hung up.

"Wallace is having breakfast at the Connaught," Stone said to Jenna.

"We did that once. He liked it there."

"Did they take his hat away from him?"

She laughed. "Yes. I hope they did so again."

"They did. Dino's there, too. He's going to let us know where Wallace goes."

"I'm hungry, but I don't want to get up," she said.

"We know how to handle that around here," Stone said, picking up the phone and ordering breakfast.

"What will we do until it comes?" she asked.

"Well, we shouldn't be actually fucking when they walk in. Can you wait until after breakfast?"

"If I have to," she said.

"Are you always like this?" Stone asked.

"Only for the last four years, or so. I have a lot of catching up to do."

———

They were on coffee when Dino called back.

"Hey."

"Hey. The senator has left the building."

"Can you be more specific?"

"Well, he's on Park Lane, in the rear seat of an elderly Rolls-Royce, as we speak. I, on the other hand, am in a mere taxi, following him."

"I don't want you to spend the day in a cab," Stone said. "If you get some idea of his direction, will you let me know before you break off?"

"Sure. We're headed west now. Just passed Harrods. I'll keep you informed."

"Is he alone?" Jenna asked.

"I forgot to ask. I will when Dino calls back."

Stone called for the removal of the dishes. He was about to attack Jenna when Dino called again.

"Okay," he said. "He drove west to that big roundabout. If you continue straight, you'll go to Heathrow, but he didn't do that."

"What did he do?"

"He got off the roundabout before the turn for the M4 and Heathrow, then drove to another roundabout and turned toward the motorway to Southampton. At that point, the cab's meter was going round and round like a slot machine. So I broke off because I don't have a lot of pounds in my pocket."

"Was anyone with him in the car?"

"Yeah, a guy wearing a black cowboy hat."

"You're a champ, Dino. I owe you all sorts of stuff."

"You remember that," Dino said, then hung up.

Stone turned back to Jenna. "He's headed this way, sort of. There's a guy in the car with him wearing a Stetson."

"What color?"

"Black."

"Oh, shit," she said.

"Who is he?"

"His name is Harley Quince."

"Who is he?"

"He's the guy Wallace calls if he wants somebody hurt," she said. "Or maybe dead."

8

Stone was mulling over what Jenna had just said.

"I'm sorry to be the bearer of bad news," Jenna said.

"Excuse me, I have to make a call." He got out his Agency-issued Apple phone and called Lance Cabot's private number.

"Don't tell me," Lance said. "You've just finished breakfast, and you wanted to wake up somebody."

"I'm sorry about that, Lance. I didn't think about the time zone."

"You're lucky that I'm already up, or I would have somebody fire a Hellfire missile at your house. What's up?"

Stone told him about the appearance of Senator Wallace Slade in London.

"That's surprising," Lance said. "I'll put a tail on him."

"You'll have to find him, first," Stone said. "He had breakfast at the Connaught this morning, where Dino also was. Dino followed him west of London, then southwest, toward Southampton."

"And you," Lance said.

"Exactly. He was accompanied by a man Jenna says is named Harley Quince, who Wallace hires for rough stuff and the occasional killing."

"Description?"

"Hang on." He turned to Jenna. "Can you describe Harley Quince?"

"About Wallace's size, but slimmer and more muscular. He has yellow hair, like Donald Trump, after his dye job."

Stone repeated that to Lance. "And he wears a black Stetson," he added. "Wallace wears a white one. That should help with IDing them both."

"How far would they be from you right now?"

"Assuming they're headed here, about an hour. They should be on the M3 motorway by now."

"What are they driving?"

"Dino says an elderly Rolls-Royce, and he has a driver."

"What does Dino mean by 'elderly'?"

"Jesus, I don't know. Not a newer model, I guess."

"Color?"

"He didn't say, and I didn't ask."

"You're both such a big help. Is Dino tailing him?"

"Not anymore. He was in a London taxi and he was out of sterling."

"What do you have by way of weapons in the house?"

"I've got a matched brace of Purdey 12-gauge double-barreled shotguns and a deer rifle with a scope."

"My advice is, use the deer rifle. Don't wait until they're close enough for the shotguns."

"That's helpful, Lance, thank you."

"What you need is a couple of Kalashnikovs."

"Well, don't send any of those here. I'd have to explain them to the police, and they might not understand."

"You've got that tame Chief Inspector Holmes around, haven't you?"

"Sort of tame. He's never bitten me, anyway."

"I think he could get men with guns there faster than I," Lance said. "We have a London station, but not a Hampshire one."

"I'll call Holmes. You call Felicity," Stone said. "The request should go to her, and not from me."

"All right," Lance said, then hung up without further ado.

"What did Lance say?" Jenna asked.

Stone picked up the phone and dialed another number. "I don't suppose you smuggled any automatic weapons into the country, did you?"

"I don't remember doing so."

"Hello, may I speak to Chief Inspector Holmes, please? My name is Stone Barrington."

"This is Holmes," a voice said sleepily. "Is that you, Barrington?"

"It is, Chief Inspector. I'm sorry to trouble you, but I'm informed that there may be men with weapons on their way to my house, with the intention of harming my houseguest, who is also a guest of the CIA."

"Oh," Holmes said drily. "I seem to get calls like this every day."

"I apologize for the inconvenience, but do you suppose you could send a few well-armed men over here?"

"Armed with what?"

"Assault rifles would be a welcome sight."

"This is not an American joke, is it?"

"It is not. I'll be happy to put you in direct contact with the director of Central Intelligence, if it would help you make a quick decision."

"How quick?"

"I'm told the assassins could be here in less than an hour."

"My word. Let me see what we've got in our wee armory and who we've got who can fire a weapon without shooting himself in the foot. I'll ring you back. You're at the Beaulieu number, are you?"

"I am."

Holmes hung up.

"What's the news?" Jenna asked.

"I'm not sure," Stone replied. "It's hard to tell with the British. They don't panic easily."

"What do we need from them?"

"Panic."

"I think I'd better get dressed, if we're hoping for panic," she said, running into her dressing room.

Stone got dressed, and went down to his study, where the gun cabinet lay.

He had just picked up the deer rifle when there was a hammering on the front door. He answered it to find two uniformed police officers and two plainclothesmen on the front steps, one of them Chief Inspector Holmes, and all of them were armed with light machine guns.

"Good morning, Stone," Holmes said. "I believe we're expected."

"Not only expected, but very welcome," Stone replied, waving them in.

Holmes looked at his wristwatch. "I see we've beaten the villains here."

"You have. Come in and let me get you some coffee." He stopped the passing butler and gave him instructions.

Shortly, the four men were arrayed in the library, their weapons on the floor beside them, drinking coffee and eating what they liked to call **biscuits**, which Stone was quite sure should be called **cookies**.

"Well," Holmes said, setting down his empty cup and consulting his watch again, "the villains are late."

Stone heard the crunch of gravel coming from the front of the house. "Aha!" he said, starting toward the front door, waving for his guests to follow him. He opened the door in time to hear something with a large engine driving away from the house and back toward the village.

"Chief Inspector," Stone said. "Perhaps when you answer a call of this nature it would be better to arrive in unmarked cars." He stepped outside and let them check out their vehicles, which were resplendent with markings related to the Hampshire Police.

"Ah, well, yes," Holmes muttered. "Make a note, Willis." Willis made a note.

"Well," Holmes said, "we seem to have achieved our purpose by merely showing up. Gentlemen, shall we?"

"If you're short of parking space back at your station," Stone said, "you're welcome to leave a car parked here for a week or so. You could park a couple of your machine guns, as well."

"I'm afraid both those requests can only be honored by the home secretary," Holmes said. "Do you know him?"

"I'm afraid not," Stone replied. He thanked them all, and they drove away. He had forgotten to mention the elderly Rolls-Royce.

9

Stone went back into the house and called Felicity.

"Good morning, dear Stone," she drawled. "Are you having an interesting day?"

"A little more interesting than I might wish," he replied. He recounted the events of the morning.

"My goodness," she said. "Do you mean to say that we have a rampaging United States senator at large in our capital city, accompanied by an assassin?"

"It would appear so." He explained Holmes's visit.

"So, your man Holmes did the right thing inadvertently?"

"I had hoped he and his men might have shot our visitors."

"Your **almost** visitors."

"Felicity, I presume that you are acquainted with the home secretary."

"He was in this office ten minutes ago, giving some foreigner a tour of our most secret rooms."

"Could you persuade him, do you think, to allow me to have possession of a few firearms?"

"In your house, or on your person?"

"Well, both."

"I suggest you have Lance call him directly. Sir John would find it too easy to say no to me."

"What a good idea."

"Have you any plans for dinner, you and the lovely Jenna?"

"No, we don't."

"Then why don't you invite me?" she said. "Say, seven, for drinks?"

"Of course. Would you like to bring Sir John?"

"I know you said that in jest, Stone, but as it happens, he's down here for the weekend. And I happen to know that his wife is visiting her ailing mother in Northumberland. He'll leap at the chance of a meal he didn't cook himself."

"Then, by all means, drag him over."

"Shall we say mess kits? Sir John loves a uniform, and he has far too few opportunities to wear one." By "mess kits," she meant the dress uniform of the Royal Yacht Squadron, to which both Stone and the home secretary belonged.

"Then let's give him a treat," Stone said. "Seven it is." He hung up and spoke to the cook about dinner.

Jenna entered the room. "Are the police gone already?" she asked.

"They accomplished part of their task all too quickly, then left," Stone replied.

"Which part of their task did they accomplish?"

"The part about scaring off the assassins. I'm afraid they arrived in liveried police cars."

"And what part did they fail to accomplish?"

"The part about shooting the assassins. Turns out, I need the authority of the home secretary to house or bear arms."

"What's a home secretary?"

"The cabinet minister in charge of the police."

"Oh."

"Not to worry, though. Felicity has invited herself to dinner, and she's bringing him with her."

"How convenient! Does he have a name?"

"Sir John."

"Is that it?"

"Rowling, I think. Oh, and we'll be black tie. Sir John likes to wear his yacht club uniform when he's down here."

"Which yacht club?"

"The Royal Yacht Squadron. It's at Cowes, on the Isle of Wight, just across the Solent."

"What's the Solent?"

"The body of the English Channel that

separates the Isle of Wight from the mainland. It's right down there." He pointed south.

"Do I get to wear a uniform, too?"

"Did you bring a uniform?"

"No. The last time I wore it was when I was a drum majorette, in high school."

"Then anything that shows some cleavage will do nicely."

"Sir John enjoys cleavage, does he?"

"Cleavage is good for morale."

"All right, so it's 'tits out' for the evening?"

"On any occasion, except, perhaps, a high Episcopal mass."

"I'll see what I can do."

"Can I watch?"

"Certainly, if you promise to get grabby."

"You can count on me."

"I thought so."

They went upstairs.

10

Felicity and Sir John Rowling arrived together, via her boat, and were driven to the house in a golf cart.

Stone greeted them in the library, where he and Felicity exchanged kisses. "You know Sir John Rowling, don't you, Stone? Sir John, Stone Barrington of New York."

"Of course," Sir John said. "We met at the Squadron, didn't we?"

"Must have been there," Stone said. He had no recollection of meeting the man.

The butler filled their drink orders, and as they were sitting down, Jenna entered the room, looking smashing, Stone thought. He introduced Sir John.

They sat by the fire, the ladies with champagne,

the gentlemen with whisky. The chat turned to Felicity's work, then she remembered that Jenna was not cleared to hear any of it.

Sir John saved the day. "Jenna," he said, looking concerned, "I believe you are an unwilling guest in our country."

"Not unwilling, Sir John, just unexpectedly. When I was put aboard Stone's airplane two days ago, I had no notion of my destination."

"Did you, Stone?" he asked.

"I did know our destination, but not our guest. I was not introduced to her until we had left United States air space, at the request of Lance Cabot."

"Well, if no one knows, no one can know, can one?"

"Quite right—or at least, I thought that was the case. But then her former husband turned up in London yesterday, looking for me."

"How did he know you were even in this country?"

"Either there was a leak somewhere or he is a very good guesser, since he and I have never met. And I am glad to keep it that way."

"Anything my office can do to help," Sir John said, but it wasn't a question, exactly.

"There is something," Stone said.

"Pray tell, what?"

"We have already had an unexpected visit from a man I believe to be her ex-husband, accompanied by a man Jenna tells me is little more than an assassin. We suddenly found ourselves unarmed and, therefore, vulnerable."

"Did you call the police?"

"I did, and they arrived just in time to frighten them into leaving."

"Well, then, you're all right."

"Not if they return."

"I see, and you wish to bear arms against them?"

"Not necessarily, but I would like to have that option—legally, of course."

"I see," Sir John said, and Stone thought he was beginning to. "And it would be helpful if I were to authorize the bearing of and the use of firearms in this house?"

"And on our persons," Stone replied. "That would solve our problem, I think."

"Felicity, do you concur?"

"I do, John. I believe it is the immediate and, perhaps, only solution."

"Very well, I can do that. Permanently or for the short term?"

"Since we don't know how short the term might be, I think permanently," Stone replied.

Sir John took a small notebook from an inside pocket. "Long or short guns?"

"Both, if at all possible."

"Will two of each do you?"

"I hope so."

"Four of each might be better," Felicity said.

"Oh, all right. I'll see that the proper document is messengered to you tomorrow morning."

"John," Felicity said, "I would worry less about the situation if the document were messengered to us this evening."

"Excuse me a moment," he said, producing a cell phone, rising, and walking to the other end of the library, then returning. "It should arrive in time for cheese," he said. "Certainly, for dessert."

"Oh, John," Felicity gushed. "I feel ever so much better for the safety of our guests."

"These things have to be done, at times," Sir John replied.

They dined on a venison stew with a stout burgundy. During the service of port and Stilton, the butler entered with an envelope. "For Sir John," he said, handing it over. "Will there be a reply?"

Sir John removed a document and read it. "Looks very official, doesn't it?" he said, handing it to Felicity for her perusal.

"It's perfect," she said.

Sir John handed it to Stone. "Oh, will you seal it, please, Sir John?" Stone took a stick of sealing wax from a nearby table and waved it over a candle, dripping wax onto the document and handing it to Sir John, who pressed his signet ring into the wax.

"You may take that into the shop of any

firearms dealer and receive service," Sir John said.

"I'm very grateful, Sir John, and I will sleep better tonight," Stone said.

Felicity took leave of them momentarily to make a phone call, then sat down and resumed drinking her port.

They passed a convivial evening, then, as the guests were leaving, Felicity whispered to Stone, "Look under your staircase," she said, then kissed him on the lips and followed Sir John to the cart.

Stone waved them off, closed the door, and leaned against it. "I have instructions to look under the staircase," he said. He opened the cupboard door there and found two 12-gauge riot guns and a box with two semiautomatic pistols and another box with ammunition.

They went to bed armed and slept soundly.

11

Senator Wallace Slade sat in the rear of the elderly Rolls-Royce, which had become his rolling office, with Harley Quince seated beside him. "Aaron," he said to his chauffeur, "stretch your legs, buddy."

"Yes, sir," the man said, then left the car.

"That didn't go well yesterday," the senator said to Quince.

"We couldn't predict them four police cars," Harley said. "'Less you want a whole lot more folks dead."

"Just one," Wallace said. "No, make that two."

"Are they colocated?" Harley asked.

"They are."

"Whaddaya have against this fella Barrington?"

"He's fucking my wife."

"He didn't even **know** your wife until a couple of days ago. And she ain't your wife no more."

"Harley," Slade said, "I like you better when you're your strong, silent self."

"All right, I'll shut up."

"At least we've found the house," Slade said.

Harley said nothing.

"We know how long it takes to drive down there, too."

Silence from Harley.

"You got any ideas?" Slade asked.

"You speakin' to me?"

"All right, Harley. I apologize. Now, give me some ideas."

"Well, I'd prefer going in there at night, when they're asleep or, in the case of your wife, fucking, and kill everybody we can find. Oh, then get outta there and go home. I'm getting tired of hearing these folks talk."

"What makes you think it would be that easy?"

"Well, this ain't Waco," Harley pointed out. "They don't carry in this country, not even the cops."

"I've seen policemen who carry," Slade said. "And if you take a stroll around Buckingham Palace, you'll see some carrying automatic weapons."

"Waaall . . ."

"These people like to shoot game, too. That means they've got a pair of shotguns in a closet that cost more than you made last year, and maybe a deer rifle or two."

"Do they sleep with 'em?" Harley asked.

"Probably not."

"Then what's wrong with my plan?"

"It may come to that," Slade said. "What I can't figure out is why there were four police cars in front of the house when we got there. How would they know we were coming?"

"Maybe they had a burglar?"

"Four police cars for a burglar is damned fine police service," Slade said.

"I won't argue with that," Harley said. "But I doubt they're there every night."

"Well, if we go down there every night this week, we'll find out, won't we?"

"Well, I could go in there by myself," Harley said, "but I'd rather have me some backup."

"Tell you what. I'll find you some backup, Harley. But if you get caught in that house, you might as well just put your gun to your head because I'm going to be in another country real fast."

"Chickenshit bastard," Harley muttered under his breath.

"I heard that. Watch your mouth."

"I'm going to need three more guys," Harley said.

"Why so many?"

"Because we don't know what we're up against, and we ain't got time to research the project. And we're probably going to have to kill more than two people."

"All right, get three more men, but tell them to bring their own weapons."

"And what are you going to be doing while we're killing those folks?"

"I'm your getaway driver."

"In a fucking Rolls-Royce? How hard is that going to be to find? And have you ever driven that thing on the wrong side of the road?"

"All right, tell me what you want, Harley. I can get what you need."

"I want every man to be English, not American, and have a sawed-off shotgun and a pocketful of buckshot shells and packin' a handgun— .45s would be nice. Two extra mags per gun."

"What transportation?"

"Two fast cars: Jags, Beemers. Quick, but not obvious. Black is good."

"You should wear masks."

"Get us some of them surgical things at the drugstore. We'll need black shirts and pants and black knit caps, too. And I want gloves on every-body before they ever touch a weapon."

"How soon?"

"Tomorrow night. We're gonna just walk the grounds for a night before we go in."

"I like the way you think, Harley."

"It's what you're payin' for."

S tone and Jenna were having breakfast. "How would you like an outing?" he asked.

"An outing?"

"Away from the house. Overnight."

"I'm not a camper," she said.

"I promise you a soft, warm bed."

"With you in it?"

"Absolutely."

"What do I need to bring with me?"

"Casual day clothes, and something for a black-tie occasion at dinner."

"I can do that," she said.

"We'll leave here at ten."

"Are we driving?"

"We're going by sea, and don't ask any more questions."

———

By ten-thirty, they were motoring down the Beaulieu River in Stone's Hinckley 43. "You can come up now," he called, and she emerged from the master cabin. "The coast is clear," he said. "And nobody would ever think to look for us where we're going."

"And where is that?"

"To the Isle of Wight." He pointed in that direction. "The village is Cowes, the yachting capital of Britain." They made a couple of turns and emerged into the Solent. "There's the island, over there," Stone said, pointing as he added throttle and picked up speed.

She looked at the instrument panel, then at Stone, who was sitting in the captain's chair with his hands in his lap. "Who's driving?"

"The autopilot," he said, pointing at a screen. "That blip is us." It got a little bumpier. "Hop up here," he said, patting the seat next to him.

"I've never seen so many boats," Jenna said.

"You should see it during Cowes Week, the biggest regatta of the year." They passed some chalk cliffs. "Those are called the Needles," he said, "though they're not pointy anymore, having been worn down by the sea."

A few minutes later they passed the Royal Yacht Squadron, with its striped awning and its array of polished brass cannon. "That's the

Castle," Stone said, "built by Henry VIII to ward off the French. Her guns were never fired in anger, though."

"There are so many cannons," she said.

"Those are used for starting and managing yacht races."

They turned into a small marina, and two boatmen took their lines and made them fast. They retrieved their luggage, and a boatman took the bags and led them to the entrance of the Squadron. A few minutes later, they were checked into a comfortable suite. Stone got into a double-breasted blue suit with black club buttons, a white shirt, and a black necktie, sporting a Squadron stickpin. They went downstairs. On the way he showed her the library, the drawing room, and the main dining room with its array of portraits of past commodores, some of them kings. Stone led her into a comfortable sitting room, where they ordered Pimm's Cups and waited for lunch to be announced.

"This is all very cozy," Jenna said.

"A good word for it. There's a big pavilion out back, where large events can be held."

A steward announced lunch, and they went into the next room and were seated by a window, with a good view of the Solent and the yachts.

"You're right," Jenna said. "We could never be found here. "Wallace wouldn't even know this place exists."

"Nor would most Americans, except yachtsmen."

"What does 'yacht' mean?"

"It's from the Dutch. It means a sailing craft designed for pleasure; that means almost everything in the harbor, from a dingy to a three-master."

"Will we go sailing while we're here?"

"I'm afraid you'll have to be content with **Indian Summer**, aboard which we arrived. I have a sailing yacht, but it hasn't been launched this year, yet."

———

After lunch they took a stroll up Cowes's High Street and looked into the shops and galleries, then sat for a while on the Parade, a large public space next to the Squadron.

"Don't look now," Jenna said, "but I just saw a man in a black cowboy hat."

"Where?"

"He just left the Parade, walking up the High Street."

"Is it Wallace's hit man?"

"I don't know, but there are no other men in black cowboy hats out here."

"Let me know if you see him again," Stone said. "Why don't we walk on back to the Squadron. He can't hide out here on the Parade."

They walked on back, and Stone looked over his shoulder a lot, but saw no black cowboy hats.

"Why were there so few people at lunch?" Jenna asked.

"It's a Tuesday afternoon. Everybody will be driving down from London and points north at the weekend. Though there should be a good crowd this evening."

Stone stopped at the Squadron gate and had a good look behind them at the Parade. No black hats.

———

They sat in the library for a while and read the papers, then they went upstairs for a nap before changing for dinner. Stone's phone rang, and he answered it. "Yes?"

"It's Major Bugg."

"Good afternoon."

"Are you on the grounds?"

"No, we took the boat across the Solent. We're staying at the Squadron."

"Just as well. We had a couple of men sniffing around over here. Americans, by their accents."

"Any of them wearing a black cowboy hat?"

"No, but there was one who didn't get out of their car who was wearing a white one. I inquired about what they were doing on the property. And they said they were just having a look around, as if the estate were some sort of tourist venue. I had to point out that it is a private estate and ask them to leave, which they did reluctantly."

"I apologize for the rudeness of my countrymen," Stone said.

"What with our guest and all, I thought you'd like to know about them."

"Thank you, Major. If you'll have a look in the cupboard under the main stairs you'll find some comforting objects. Feel free to load one and carry it around."

"Mr. Barrington, are we licensed for that?"

"We are. If you'll look on the table in the library, you'll find a document to that effect—signed and sealed by the home secretary. Dame Felicity brought him to dinner last evening."

"I may take you up on that," Bugg said, then hung up.

"What was that about?" Jenna asked.

"Some American tourists giving themselves a tour of the property," Stone said. "They made Bugg nervous." He didn't tell her about the man in the car, wearing a white cowboy hat.

13

They had drinks on the front terrace and chatted with other dinner guests. When dinner was announced, they were shown to seats at the center table, which could be expanded from four to twelve seats. Stone reckoned there were eight at the table that evening.

A man of about sixty was seated to Stone's left, and they introduced themselves.

"You're an American, are you?" the man asked. "But you're a member here?"

Stone thought that was obvious, given his uniform. "Yes, I have a house on the Beaulieu River, Windward Manor."

"I know the place. I knew the former owner; God rest his soul."

"Yes, I bought the place from him a few months

before his death, but he remained in residence until then."

"Have you done much with the place?"

"No, it underwent a major renovation just before I bought it. It's in about as perfect condition as a house could be, I think."

"What work do you do?" the man asked.

"I'm an attorney, with the firm of Woodman & Weld, in New York."

"I know them. That fellow Eggers."

"Yes, we were at law school together. He brought me aboard."

"I'm a Lord Justice," he said, "something like a supreme court justice in your country."

"I'll tell Bill Eggers I saw you."

"Many Americans are such nice people, but I saw a man being given lunch in the House of Lords dining room yesterday, and he was wearing, of all things, a cowboy hat, like in the pictures. I inquired of the manager why he had not been thrown out and was told he was an American senator. Can you imagine?"

"I'm afraid I can," Stone said. "My dinner guest was once married to him, and he appears to be trying to track her down over here. We've had to take steps at my house."

"I hope the steps include a good twelve-bore," the man said. "That's what the fellow deserves, turning up at the House of Lords dressed like that."

"I have a very nice brace of Purdeys," Stone said.

"Ha! Just the thing for him!"

"I hope it won't come to that, but you never know these days."

"A man who would come to the House of Lords in a cowboy hat deserves whatever he gets. And if you came before my bench, I would dismiss the charges immediately!"

"That's comforting to know," Stone said. "If they come for me, I'll mention it to my barrister." On second thought Stone thought he knew somebody better to mention it to. After dinner, he called Dino at the Connaught.

"Bacchetti."

"We're expecting you tomorrow," Stone said.

"In the afternoon. Where are you? I hear babble."

"That's called conversation over here. We're at the Squadron, and I heard something that I thought that fellow at Page Six should know."

"Henry what's-his-name?"

"The very one. My dinner companion, a member of the House of Lords, told me that yesterday he saw a man in a cowboy hat having lunch in their dining room. He was outraged!"

"That sounds like our boy," Dino said. "It's early yet in New York. I'll give him a ring."

"You do that. Let's see how long it takes to resonate."

"See you tomorrow." They hung up.

Stone and Jenna had their port and Stilton and turned in fairly early. He told her about his conversation at the table.

"Exactly like him!" she said. "The man is an embarrassment to everybody he knows!"

———

They rose fairly early, packed, breakfasted, and motored out into the Solent. Stone had an uneasy feeling about being away from the house, and he wanted to get back early. They cruised up the Beaulieu and tied up at his dock, then drove a golf cart up to the house. Major Bugg met them on the front steps.

"I'm glad you're back," he said. "I spent the night on a cot in the library and walked regular rounds with one of your new shotguns. Everything was all right. But I feel better with you in residence."

"Thank you, Major," Stone said. "Mr. and Mrs. Bacchetti will be back this morning. We'll have dinner at seven. Please let Cook know."

"Of course."

"Now, you go home and get some good sleep."

Bugg put away his shotgun and left the house.

———

Dino and Viv arrived in the Range Rover with the London papers. One of the tabloids featured a photograph of Wallace Slade lunching, à la Stetson, at the House of Lords. "U.S. Senator Outrages Lords!" the headline shouted.

Stone grinned broadly. "Anything in the **International New York Times**?"

"Not yet. Maybe tomorrow."

"You two need a nap after your drive," Stone said. "Drinks at six-thirty. No need to dress, it's just us."

"See you then," Dino said, and they went upstairs.

Stone and Jenna went upstairs to nap, too, and ended up not napping.

14

Stone's phone rang at mid-morning. "Hello?"

"It's Lance," he said in his smooth baritone.

"Good morning."

"I saw your little shot at Wallace Slade in today's **New York Post**. Very nice. It's being picked up by the TV news people and will probably feature on the Sunday shows this weekend."

"Excellent," Stone replied. "I didn't know it would work to such good effect."

"Somebody stuck a microphone in Slade's face, and his comment was: 'Them Limeys don't git Texans.'"

"Perfect. He insults the English and Texans in one fell swoop. By the way, good accent."

"I thought that, too. How are you and Jenna getting along?" Lance asked.

"Quite nicely, thank you."

"She's now scheduled to testify before the committee on Monday morning at nine, in New York. They're investigating something else up there and want to grab her testimony while they're at it, so you'd better have her back on Sunday evening."

"I think we can manage that."

"I understand you had dinner with one of the law lords last night."

"News travels fast," Stone said. "It's almost as if you were head of the CIA or something."

"One hears things."

"Where do I have to deliver Jenna on Monday morning?"

"The committee is meeting at the New York Public Library, at Fifth Avenue and Forty-Second Street." He gave Stone a room number. "I'd be there half an hour early if I were you. And don't come armed. You'll just be searched and stripped of it."

"I assume there'll be others there who will be armed and playing on our team," Stone said.

"A fair assumption. C-SPAN is televising the hearing, so I'll be tuned in."

"I'll ask Jenna to wave at you."

"You do that." Lance hung up.

"Was that Lance?" Jenna asked.

"Yes, and the news is good. You're testifying Monday morning in New York."

"How convenient," she said. "I assume you won't deny me shelter there."

"Nor sustenance," Stone replied. "Shall we fly on Sunday, or do you have shopping to do in preparation for the hearing?"

"I do. May we fly on Friday? Then I'll have Saturday to sack the shops."

"I'll order the airplane for Friday." He passed the news on to Dino and Viv and called Faith to give her instructions.

———

Before cocktails, Stone moved the firearms to the gun cabinet in the library and loaded all the weapons. Leaving their safeties on.

"Did you leave one up the spout?" Dino asked, when Stone pointed out their location.

"No, I think the sound of a pump shotgun being racked could be a useful deterrent."

"Quite right," Dino agreed.

Thus armed, they sat down to dinner.

———

After dinner, Stone and Jenna rolled in the hay for a while. When she was asleep—sex rendered Jenna, like a man, unconscious—he got into some dark clothes and met Dino downstairs, at the gun cabinet. They each took a riot gun, and they both already carried a handgun.

"All right," Stone said, "you go out the back door and turn left. I'll go out the front and turn right. We'll meet on the west side of the house, then continue around the perimeter, say three rounds."

"Okay," Dino said.

They filled their pockets with shells and magazines and started for their respective doors. "Oh, Dino," Stone said, as they walked away from each other.

"Yeah?"

"If you shoot **me**, I'll be really pissed off."

"Gotcha."

———

Stone walked out the front door and closed it quietly behind him. He stood on the front porch and looked around, letting his eyes become accustomed to the darkness. When he could see as much as he expected to see, he walked down the front steps to the driveway and started walking, visually sweeping the area.

A car drove past the front gate and continued south, without slowing, and Stone paid no further attention to it. At the corner of the house, he stopped and made a slow, 360-degree turn, looking and listening as hard as he could.

Nothing. He continued slowly around the corner and began to pay attention to the shrubs and flower beds.

"Bang! You're dead!" Dino said, causing Stone to jump about a foot.

Stone turned and found him sitting on a wrought-iron bench.

"That wasn't funny," he said.

"Are you kidding me? It was hilarious."

"If you aren't careful, you're going to end up with a snoot full of buckshot."

"You know," Dino said, "if we continue these circuits, we'll just make ourselves tired. Let's just sit here for a while and let them come to us."

"Good idea," Stone said, sitting down next to him.

They were quiet for a while, then Dino said, "So, after Jenna testifies on Monday, this is over, right?"

"I suppose so. I don't see how drawing this out can be good for Wallace Slade."

"Neither can I. Have you noticed how hard it is to use the title 'Senator' in front of his name? I just can't manage it."

"I know what you mean."

"Jenna is a sweet kid," Dino said.

"If you consider forty a kid, then she is."

"If they're cute, they're a kid," Dino said.

"I'm sure there's an organization somewhere that would have you publicly drawn and quartered for saying that."

"Yeah, but their reach doesn't extend to an iron bench in the garden at Windward Hall."

"You have a point, but don't start letting yourself talk that way."

"I've always talked that way."

"I know that, but if you talk that way anywhere near a TV camera in New York, you'll find yourself in early retirement."

"Point taken. I'll make an effort to mend my ways."

Dead ahead of them, in the shrubbery, there was a loud, scrambling noise. They each dove in a different direction, racking their shotguns as they flew through the air.

Stone landed and stayed perfectly still. Then a large shape emerged from the bushes, and to Stone's shock, it made a mooing noise.

"Shit!" Dino yelled. "Do you keep cows here?"

"No," Stone replied. "It must have wandered in from a neighbor's place. He'll probably come looking for it in the morning."

"Well, that's enough excitement for me for one night," Dino said, standing and brushing himself off. "I'm turning in."

"I guess I will, too," Stone said.

"And if that cow has any complaints, we're going to have steak for dinner tonight," Dino said.

15

Stone was awakened shortly after dawn by Jenna, who was in need. He satisfied her as best he could.

"That was wonderful," she said, nestling close.

"I do my best," he replied.

"Your best is just perfect."

"Thank you, ma'am."

They fell asleep again, until Stone was wakened by his cell phone. "Yes?"

"It's Felicity."

"Well, good morning."

"I understand Mr. Slade took an arrow in the chest," she said, "so to speak."

"I'm glad you've heard, and I hope the rest of the world has, too. Lance saw it in the **New York Post**."

"The perfect spot for it."

"We're off for New York tomorrow. Jenna is testifying at a hearing there on Monday morning."

"Oh, I'm so sorry you're leaving before I got to know her better," Felicity said slyly.

"Oh, well."

"But you're still there tonight?"

"We are."

"Perhaps you could ask if she has an interest in seeing me for dinner?"

"I can ask."

"Call me back." She hung up.

Jenna stirred beside him. "Have we had breakfast yet?"

"No, I'll order it up." He did so.

When she was fully awake, he tried to sound casual. "Do you recall that I mentioned Felicity's carnal interests?"

"I seem to remember."

"Does that interest you in any way?"

"Well, it's a thought. Does this include you, as well?"

"It's been my experience with threesomes that the women tend to be more interested in each other than in me."

"Oh, poor baby! I wouldn't allow that to happen."

"Tonight is our last one here for a while, and Felicity has hinted that she would like to be asked to dinner, and so forth."

"Oh, dinner **and** so forth! Is that how she put it?"

"As I recall, she was a bit more direct than that."

"She likes me?"

"She does."

"Actually, I noticed that at our first meeting."

"Did you? That was very astute."

"It was hard to miss. She looks at me the way I look at you, at times."

"What is your wish?"

"Will I like her?"

"That's entirely up to you."

"All right, let me put it this way: Do **you** like her?"

"In bed?"

"That's what we're talking about, isn't it?"

"Yes. She's very . . . accommodating."

"Then invite her," Jenna said. "I'll see that you're not ignored."

Stone laughed "That's a kind thought."

———

Dinner was over, and the fire was burning low. Dino and Viv excused themselves and went to bed. Felicity moved from her chair to the sofa, next to Jenna. She put a hand on Jenna's cheek and stroked it, then kissed her lightly, then ran a finger down her cleavage. "Stone," she said, "I seem to recall that there is a bed in this house."

"There is indeed. A big one."

"Then let's go find it."

They went upstairs to the master suite, and clothing was made to disappear. They got into bed with Jenna between them, and everyone's breathing grew faster.

He had to wait for a bit, but Stone, to his delight, was not ignored by either of them.

With everyone gratified, they slept. Then, near dawn, they awakened and started over.

———

At mid-morning, the G-500 began its takeoff roll, then lifted off. Jenna, at the window, waved. "Goodbye, Windward Hall," she said.

"Don't worry," Stone said, "the two of you will meet again."

"It can't be too soon for me," she said. "By the way, last night was lovely. I felt pampered."

Stone laughed. "So did I."

———

With the time difference, they landed at Teterboro in the early afternoon. Fred was there with the Bentley, while Dino's official car drove the Bacchettis home.

———

"Mr. Barrington," Fred said, when they were clear of the airport, "I thought you'd like to know, the house is well-stocked with security folk."

"Then Strategic Services is doing its work."

Fred handed them a two-day-old **Post**. "I saved this for you."

They read the newspaper account of Slade's gaffe. "Very interesting," Stone said. "Thank you, Fred, I hope to read more like that."

"We have only to wait," Jenna said. "Wallace will not disappoint us."

"Do you think he'll turn up at the hearing?"

"I shouldn't think so. What will be said about him will be humiliating. I expect he'll have someone there, though."

"He won't need to," Stone said. "Lance told me it will be on C-SPAN."

She smiled. "Oh, good."

16

Stone and Jenna had a talk about the hearing, and they decided to send her to the library in a rented car with a driver. He did not think it a good idea for him to escort her or to even send her in his own car. After all, they might need to leave town again, and he wanted no one to draw the conclusion that he was the person hiding her.

Stone tuned in to C-SPAN and watched the two-hour hearing. Jenna made her opening statement without notes, then took questions. Her answers were brief and to the point. The Republicans on the committee, led by the senior senator from Texas, tried to give her a hard time and, largely, failed. Jenna maintained her composure, and even scored some points.

Then, during a brief wide shot of the hearing room, Stone spotted a black cowboy hat. Slade was, indeed, represented in the room. Stone called Mike Freeman.

"Yes, Stone?"

"Are you watching the hearing?"

"Sort of, but I'm also doing the crossword."

"There's a man wearing a black Stetson in the audience. He is Slade's enforcer, perhaps even assassin."

"I've stopped doing the crossword now," Mike said.

"Please contact the head of your detail and have him or her put four people into the audience and place them as closely as possible to the hat. The man's name is Harley Quince, and I want him to know that we're on him, so tell them to crowd him."

"Consider it done."

"Then call the head of security for the committee and ask him to brace Quince at the earliest opportunity and check him for ID and weapons that might not have set off a metal detector. Then get Jenna into her car and out of there. If you can, send a vehicle to follow her that can block any tail, if necessary. When she's clear of all tails, then drive her into my garage and deposit her there. Tell the driver of her car to wait a few minutes before departing the garage."

"Got it," Mike said.

"Are you free for dinner this evening?"

"Yes."

"Come here, drinks at six-thirty, and bring a date. Do you own a necktie?"

"I do."

"Wear it."

"Love to."

They said goodbye and hung up. Stone waited for another wide shot of the room, and it was a while coming, but when it did, Stone saw four men sitting close to Quince who hadn't been there before. He smiled at the sight. He called Dino and invited him and Viv to dinner as well. Then he called Lance Cabot.

"Yes, Stone?"

"Are you available in New York for dinner at my house?"

"I am. Black tie?"

"Just a tie," Stone replied. "Did you watch the hearing?"

"As much of it as I could."

"Jenna did well, don't you think?"

"She did. I was proud of her."

"When is Slade going to be arrested?"

"That's complicated. After all, the man is a sitting United States senator. The papers and the TV shows will be all over him, though."

"I'd like to see him in prison."

"So would a lot of people, and that could happen yet. We need more than Jenna's testimony.

The Texans are already calling her a woman scorned."

"That had to happen. See you at six-thirty for drinks. Oh, will you be bringing anyone?"

"Probably not, but maybe I'll get lucky." They both hung up. Stone called Helene and told her to prepare for another guest.

———

Stone got a call later: "Mike Freeman is my boss. I'm in your garage."

"I'll be right there." He went to the garage and opened the rear door of a black-on-black limo. Jenna fell into his arms, and she was trembling.

"What's wrong?" Stone asked, but she was gasping for breath. He rapped sharply on the driver's window, and the darkened glass slid down. "What happened?"

"We picked up a tail—guy in a black cowboy hat. We lost him, but the incident upset her."

"Okay, get going," Stone said, pressing the remote to open the garage door. The limo drove out and away, followed by two other vehicles.

Stone held Jenna close. "It's all right. You're safe."

She finally could draw a deep breath. "It was Quince," she said.

"I know, but they lost him, so he didn't follow you here." He steered her inside and gave her a drink, stayed with her until she calmed down, then sent her upstairs.

———

When Lance entered the house that night, he took Stone aside. "I have good news," he said.

"I can always use some of that."

"The FBI has concentrated its investigation of Senator Slade. They've put a heavy and very noticeable detail on him, to make him nervous."

"Tell them they need to put a separate detail on Harley Quince, he of the black Stetson. He's dangerous."

"The good news is they already have. The bad news is they've already lost him."

"Oh, swell."

"They'll find him, eventually."

"I hope 'eventually' is soon enough."

"So do I."

Stone double-locked the front door, and they went into the living room for drinks. "I found this guy wandering around the neighborhood, looking lost," he said to the group, "so I invited him to dinner." Then Stone said, "He works for the government, so keep your hand on your wallet."

17

They had drinks and were seated for dinner before anyone noticed that Jenna wasn't saying much.

"I watched on C-SPAN," Viv said to her. "You did very well."

Jenna shrugged. "I was doing all right until I saw the black Stetson in the audience, then I got a little rattled."

"Nobody noticed," Stone said. "That's why Quince was there, to rattle you, and it didn't work."

"I hope you're right," she said, and began to cheer up.

"So, Lance," Stone said, "tell us the latest on the investigation into Wallace Slade."

"That's the FBI's case," Lance replied. "We come in only if we're asked."

"Have you been asked?"

"In small ways. The Feds haven't asked us to shoot him."

"A pity," Stone said.

"Yes, it would be lots of fun, wouldn't it?"

"Slade might be a good class project for the current crop of trainees at the Farm," Stone suggested.

"I know you meant that to be funny, Stone," Lance replied, "but it's rather a good idea. It would give them some real-time experience, and it would scare the hell out of Slade, to see a bunch of kids in the bushes wherever he goes."

Everyone chuckled.

"I'll see to it tomorrow morning," Lance said.

Dino had been uncharacteristically quiet. "What are the chances of pinning a major felony on Slade?"

"Fair to good, I should think. A few years in a room with bars would be character-building for him."

Stone spoke up. "I was thinking more, like, Guantánamo. The balmy breezes might suit him better."

"What a good idea!" Lance said. "Give him an opportunity to polish his Arabic."

———

As Stone and Jenna got into bed, she snuggled close. "This is what I thought about today when I got rattled," she said. "And it calmed my nerves."

A burst of loud noise from the street made her hold him tighter. "Small-arms fire?" she asked.

"Firecrackers," Stone replied. "Once in a while the local kids get ahold of some, and they want everybody to know it."

He did what he could to make her forget the noise.

———

Jenna was in the shower the following morning when Stone's phone rang. "Hello?"

"It's Lance. We didn't have an opportunity to get into it last night, but I want to let you know where things stand."

"Tell me."

"Jenna's testimony had the desired effect on Slade, but it has also created a backlash. Where Slade was angry before, he is now explosively furious. That is not what we want, and it's not good for Jenna. I don't think she should remain in New York. It might be too easy for Quince to find her."

"What do you suggest?" Stone asked.

"Somewhere else."

"Would you care to be more specific?"

"Paris, L.A., Key West, Maine?" Stone had houses in all those places.

"You're still paying for the airplane?"

"Yes. I've already sent you a check for the last flights."

"Maine might be the best choice. It's cooler, and it's easier to spot strange visitors than somewhere like Key West, where everybody is strange."

"I tend to agree."

"How soon?"

"The day before yesterday?"

"I'll call you later."

He lay back on the bed and waited for Jenna to emerge from the bathroom. When she did, she was naked. She knelt on the bed.

"Was that Lance?"

"It was."

"What does he want me to do?"

"Disappear from New York and reappear in Maine."

"I've never been to Maine. What's it like?"

"Cool, green, and beautiful."

"Sold! When do we go?"

He checked his watch. "This afternoon? Wheels up at two?"

"What sort of clothes do I need?"

"Think L.L.Bean."

"Tweedy stuff?"

"Good. And cashmere sweaters. You can shop the catalogs for anything you need."

"Then let's do it." She went to get dressed and pack.

Stone started making the preparatory phone calls, including one to Dino. "I don't suppose you're up for Maine," he said.

"Always, but it depends on when."

"Wheels up at two PM?"

"I can't do that, but I can catch up with you this weekend. Viv will be God-knows-where."

"Done. I've got more calls to make."

———

The G-500 set down at Rockland airport, where Stone's Cessna 182 was waiting for the short flight to the Islesboro Airport, which had too short a runway for the Gulfstream. Faith hangared the G-500 and locked the door.

Seth Hotchkiss, Stone's caretaker, met them at Islesboro's little airport in the beautifully restored 1938 Ford woodie station wagon that was Stone's local car, and they were at the house ten minutes later.

———

Jenna unpacked, then came back downstairs in time for drinks. "So, how do you come to own this house?"

"I'll try to make a long story short. I had a first cousin, Dick Stone, who built the place for himself, his wife, and their daughter. Sadly, they were all shot to death shortly after they moved in, and I inherited a lifetime occupancy, the title being left to a charity. I bought the house from the charity and have been here ever since."

"I think you skipped a lot of details," she said.

"I'll explain as they come up," he replied. "There's a friend, Ed Rawls, coming for dinner with his current girlfriend. He specializes in attractive widows."

"Oh, good."

"Something else you should know: Dick Stone was CIA and had just gotten a big promotion when he died. Ed was CIA, too, and there are a few other Agency retirees on the island."

"I'll keep that in mind. If they're all as nice as Lance . . ."

"Oh, nicer."

The doorbell rang, and Stone opened the front door to find Ed Rawls standing there. "You're early," he said. "It's only five o'clock."

"That's not why I'm here," Rawls said. "I suppose, since it's you, there will be people looking for you."

"That's possible," Stone admitted.

"They're already here," Rawls said.

18

Stone was dismayed. "Who? Where?"

"The people who are looking for you. They're all over the place."

"Come in, Ed," Stone said, pulling him inside and closing the door behind him. "Ed, this is Jenna Jacoby."

"Hi," Ed said. "I've seen you somewhere."

"Hi, Ed. I have that kind of face."

"Don't change the subject, Ed," Stone said. "Who are these people and where?"

"How the hell should I know where they are?" Ed demanded. "You'd know that."

"Once again, where are they?"

"Everywhere. Two of them followed me here. They're across the road in the bushes."

"How are they traveling?"

"Bicycles, mostly."

"Bicycles? There aren't all that many on the island."

"You can rent them at the village store."

"Oh, yeah. Tell me more."

"What's to tell? I can't figure this out for you, Stone."

"Are they wearing hats?"

"Yeah, most of them."

"Are the hats Stetsons?"

"Stetsons?"

"Like, cowboy hats."

"Hell, I don't know. Two of them were wearing baseball caps."

"Baseball?"

"Yankees, Red Sox. Like that."

"No cowboys?"

"Not that I've seen."

Stone had a thought. "How old are they?"

"I didn't ask," Ed replied.

"Old? Young? In between?"

"Youngish, I guess."

Stone sighed with relief.

"Why are you relieved?" Ed asked. "I wouldn't be relieved, if I were you."

"They're Lance's," Stone replied.

"Lance's?"

"That's right. From the Farm. Trainees. I suggested that he put them on warding off Wallace Slade."

"The guy from Texas? Congressman?"

"Senator."

Stone's phone rang. "Yes?"

"It's Lance. Have you seen any of my trainees?"

"Ed Rawls has. I think he wanted to shoot them."

"Why would Ed want to do that?"

"Ed doesn't like lurking. Your people are lurking, and Ed very kindly reported it to me."

"Is Ed there?"

"Yes."

"Let me speak to him."

Stone handed Ed the phone. "Lance, for you."

Ed took the phone. "Yeah? Hi, Lance. Yes, I saw them lurking. Okay, I won't shoot them. Bye." He handed the phone back to Stone.

"Get that all sorted out, Lance?"

"Yes, thank you."

"You might tell their instructor to work on their lurking."

Lance hung up.

"What do I do if I see more of them?" Ed asked.

"Yell 'BOO!!!'"

"See you at six-thirty." Rawls left.

Stone got Jenna and himself a drink and sat down. "Sorry about that. Ed is hyper-watchful; they taught him that at the Farm."

"Which farm?"

"The CIA training farm. Remember, last night

I suggested to Lance, in jest, that he should put the trainees onto dealing with Wallace?"

"Oh, yes."

"He has already done so."

"And they're lurking?"

"How did you know that?"

———

Ed Rawls showed up promptly at six-thirty with a handsome woman named Rena Pierce—Stone guessed her to be in her late fifties. She was introduced to Jenna and the two of them were given drinks.

"Spot any more lurkers?" Jenna asked.

"It's getting dark, and it's harder to see the lurkers," Ed replied. He turned toward Stone. "There's somebody missing. Where's Dino?"

"Back at his office, pretending to work," Stone replied. "He might join us at the weekend."

The doorbell rang.

"Expecting somebody else?" Ed asked.

"No," Stone replied.

Ed went and stood beside the door, one hand under his jacket.

"Don't shoot whoever it is, Ed. After all, it could just be a lurker."

"Okay."

Stone opened the door, and Lance walked in. "Evening, all," he said, shaking hands.

"Lance," Stone said. "When you called, where were you?"

"On the chopper."

"Of course."

"My business was done in New York, and I figured the flight here isn't any farther than Virginia, so I came in search of lobster."

"I'll tell Mary," Stone said, and he did. They always had lobster on their first night in Maine.

Lance accepted a drink. "Ed, seen any more of my lurkers?"

"It got dark," Ed replied.

"This is not as crazy as it sounds, Stone," Lance said.

"How the hell would Slade find us here?"

Lance turned to Jenna. "Jenna, did you call anyone after you got here?"

"I spoke to my sister, in Washington."

Stone slumped. "I'm sorry, Lance. I forgot to tell her not to use her cell phone."

"It was only my sister," Jenna said. "What's the problem?"

"May I see your cell phone, please?"

Jenna dug it out of her purse and handed it to Stone, who who tinkered around with it and gave it back to her.

"If you want to speak to anyone not present, please use the landline," Stone said. "Cell phones are easy to track."

"Oh, my God," Jenna muttered.

"My fault. I should have explained that to you."

"Do you think Wallace is smart enough to trace me?"

Lance spoke up. "Wallace knows someone who is."

"Oh."

"Ed," Lance said. "Continue to be vigilant about lurkers. If you see any wearing black Stetsons, you can shoot them."

"Gotcha," Ed replied.

———

Aided by their before-dinner drinks and a couple of bottles of a good California chardonnay, the party grew jolly. Rena Pierce turned out to be a good value, and Lance was more cheerful than he usually was.

After dinner, Stone lit a fire, and they gathered around the hearth with brandy and liqueurs.

"Where are all those kids of yours sleeping, Lance?" Stone asked.

"Not my problem; probably on the cold, wet ground."

"Not to disappoint you, Lance," Ed said, "but I left my barn open with a note on the door, welcoming them."

"Is there a toilet?" Lance asked.

"There is, as long as they shit in the woods," Rawls replied.

"Oh, Ed!" Rena said.

"That's better than in my barn."

"I grant you that," she replied.

"You're interfering with their training," Lance said. "Shelter was not part of their assignment, not to mention plumbing."

"I would have thought that the Agency would have outgrown the Boy Scout stage," Rawls said. "There are cheap motels everywhere these days. Though not on this island, now that I think of it."

"I believe they arrived here by boat," Lance said. "Perhaps it was enough of a boat to offer them shelter and a toilet."

"If that's true, then I retract my comments about the Agency," Rawls said.

"Retraction accepted." Lance poured himself another cognac.

"I don't think I would have enjoyed training at the Farm," Stone said.

"It beats Parris Island," Rawls said. "And you learn some nifty life skills like safecracking and killing with your thumb."

"How do you kill with your thumb?" Jenna asked.

"Don't ask," Lance said. "You'll have dreams about it, and we don't want that, do we?"

"I have dreams—bad ones—about Harley Quince," Jenna said.

"He will be excised from your dreams at the earliest opportunity," Lance replied.

"Is that permission to proceed?" Ed asked.

"It is not. Anyway, you don't need my permission to do anything, Ed. You're an OAP, now."

"What's an OAP?" Rena asked.

"An old-age pensioner," Ed replied. "I try not to think about that these days. That's why I like to off somebody now and then. Keeps the mind alive."

"Not the other guy's mind," Stone pointed out.

"That's the point, isn't it?"

There was a loud whacking sound from the front of the house.

"What was that?" Jenna asked.

Stone threw himself at Jenna, knocking her chair over with her in it. "Hit the deck, everybody!" he shouted, and everybody did. "That," Stone said, "was the sound of a penetrating object, striking an impenetrable surface." He reached for the nearest lamp cord and yanked it out of the wall socket. The room went dark.

All the men began to move.

19

After a few moments of them lying still, a boat's engine was heard starting up in the bay and rapidly moving away, becoming fainter.

"I think the coast is clear, as people used to say," Lance said. "Let's have some lights."

Stone plugged in the lamp he had yanked, and other lights came on, too. He got up and followed Lance out onto the front deck. Lance had produced a tiny flashlight with a powerful beam and was casting it about.

"Here we go," Lance said, illuminating a place where a chunk of the picture window was missing.

"It stood up well," Stone said, examining the chunk, which was half the size of his fist.

"That's grade-six armored glass," Lance said.

"It wasn't quite good enough," Stone replied.

"It stopped an armor-piercing bullet," Lance said.

"But just barely."

"I'll have it replaced tomorrow with a thicker pane," Lance said.

"That's already been done once," Stone said. "After Jim Hickock was shot." This was some time back.

"They're improving that stuff all the time," Lance said.

Ed Rawls joined them and examined the glass. "Lurkers?"

"Not mine," Lance said. "Somebody else's. They've fled the scene by sea."

"I'll have a look around in my boat tomorrow," Ed said.

"You will not be alone," Lance replied. "We'll have a look at every craft on the island."

"You'll need a fleet for that."

"I have a fleet."

"Well, the Agency has become a lot more nautical since my day," Rawls replied.

"Your day isn't over, Ed," Lance replied. "Not as long as you can shoot a lurker."

"I'm going to start carrying a long gun everywhere," Ed said.

"A good policy in times such as these."

"I think I'll start staying home evenings, too."

"I can't argue with that."

"Where do you think that boat is now?" Stone asked.

"Headed for Camden or Rockland, I should think," Lance said. "They won't hang around here so Ed can shoot them."

"I guess I'm going to have to start taking Wallace Slade more seriously," Stone said.

"Take Harley Quince more seriously," Lance replied. "Slade has already given him his orders and retired from the scene. His face is a lot more famous since his photograph appeared in the papers and on TV."

"Maybe that wasn't such a good idea," Stone said.

"I thought it was a good idea," Lance said. "I still do. May I borrow a bed? My chopper pilot is already asleep in the rear cabin, I should think."

"Take the guesthouse," Stone said. "Two rooms out there, both with locks on the doors and hard glass in the windows. You may invite your pilot, if you'd like to drive out and get him. There's a station wagon in the garage, and the keys are in the ignition."

"Can you loan me a long gun?"

Stone took him back inside and entered the lock combination to get into Dick Stone's concealed office. He ushered Lance inside and waved at a wall. "Take your pick. Spare magazines and ammo are on the shelves underneath."

They each took down an assault rifle and loaded up.

———

As they got into bed, Jenna said, "I'm sorry about making the phone call."

"It's my fault for not explaining it to you." Stone laid the assault rifle on the floor, on his side of the bed.

"Are we going to have to go somewhere else now?"

"No," Stone replied. "We're dug in here, and we're not going anywhere else unless Harley Quince is dead. Wallace, too, if we get the chance."

They fell asleep without having made love; a first.

———

Stone woke before sunrise, showered, shaved, and dressed. Then he picked up his rifle and went downstairs, where Mary was already making breakfast.

At sunup, Stone was walking his property, checking every patch of woods or shrubbery. He went back inside the house and found Jenna having breakfast.

"You were angry last night, weren't you?" she asked.

"I still am," Stone said, "but never at you. Not in the least."

They were shortly joined by Lance, who stood his rifle in a corner, then sat down.

"I've already walked the property," Stone said.

"Good, saves me the trouble."

"Do you want your pilot to have some breakfast?"

"I spoke to Seth. He's carrying it out to him on the field, assuming he's still alive."

Seth returned shortly and gave him a thumbs-up. "All is well," he said, handing Stone the newspapers.

Stone shared them with Lance, then went to sit by the fireplace. "Excellent editorial about Wallace Slade and the testimony at the hearings," Stone said. "Stops just short of demanding his resignation from the Senate."

"Well, we know that the Republicans will never expel him," Lance said. "Any mention of Quince?"

"It says that Slade employs thugs to deal with his enemies."

"The hearings aren't over yet, except for Jenna's testimony, which was damaging to Slade. Though, as we have seen, not fatal. I'll see that a couple of the Sunday-morning TV shows mention last night's attempt."

"It can't do any harm," Stone said, "since they already know where Jenna is. But don't mention the name of the island. The neighbors don't like TV cameras."

"Right. What are you going to do?" Lance asked.

"Stay here and hope I get a shot at somebody. You want to stay on for a long weekend?"

"I'll need to make some calls before I'll know."

"No rush. The guesthouse will still be there. And don't make your pilot sleep in the chopper."

20

They had just finished breakfast when the doorbell rang. Stone found Ed Rawls waiting there.

"Good morning, Ed, come in."

Ed came in. "I started out at first light and circumnavigated the island," he said. "I didn't find any boat that I don't know, so I suspect Lance was right. The shooter headed for more heavily trafficked waters like Camden or Rockport."

"Okay," Stone said. "You must be ready for some breakfast."

"I've eaten, but I'd love some coffee."

Stone motioned him to the table, where the pot awaited him.

Stone was about to take a seat and continue

reading the papers when the doorbell rang again. He set aside the papers and answered it. A woman in her late thirties, wearing L.L.Bean's finest everything, stood there. "Mr. Barrington, I'm Betty Black, from the Farm. May I speak to Mr. Cabot, please?"

"Sure, come in." He directed her to the table, where she declined breakfast but accepted coffee. She and Lance greeted each other. "The news is out about last night," she said.

"How did you hear?" Lance asked.

"It was all the talk at the village store. Sir, you didn't specify that you wanted my class armed, but they've all completed the small-arms course, and they're all certified. I've got a half dozen shotguns on our boat. Would you like me to order more?"

"Yes, order an assault rifle and a sidearm for each man—or whoever. I've ordered a piece of armored glass to replace the one broken last night. Ask them to fly your load up here in the same DC-3 and land on the local strip. They can call me from there, and I'll have them met. Order ammo, too. Tonight, we'll distribute your people around the island. If we're lucky, maybe we can get them some shooting experience."

"You mean at real people?"

"Yes, but we'll have a briefing for them about which real people and how to avoid shooting the locals and the summer folk, who react poorly to that sort of thing." Lance set down his coffee cup.

"Yes, sir."

"Where did your people sleep last night?"

"On the motor yacht we chartered. We were fairly comfortable."

"Order mattresses, blankets, and sleeping bags, too, if you need them. They can be flown up with the weapons."

"Yes, sir." She left the house.

"Stone, can your man meet the airplane in your station wagon?"

"Sure, have them call on touchdown."

Stone turned to Ed Rawls. "Ed, if you were on the other side of this thing, what would you do tonight?"

"I'd have another go," Rawls said, "on the premise that you wouldn't be expecting it."

"So would I, in their shoes," Stone said. "We'll be ready." He stood up. "Anybody like to take a drive around the island? It's a beautiful day, and I don't think there will be assassins about until it's dark."

Stone, Jenna, Ed, and Lance got into the station wagon and drove south.

"Gorgeous wagon," Lance said.

"Thank you. Seth works all winter on it."

They circumnavigated the island, then ended

up at the village store and got ice cream for everybody.

———

Late in the afternoon a DC-3 buzzed the house, then flew away toward the airfield. Seth had borrowed a truck, and he took it out there for the unloading of the glass, the weapons, and the bedding.

Stone had a look at the glass. "It's at least an inch thicker than the original," he said to Lance.

"Would you have preferred thinner?" Lance asked.

"I think not."

The glass was installed before sunset. The pilots and workmen returned to the airfield and took off for home.

Stone had them leave the old piece of glass leaning on the side of the garage.

Betty Black brought her plan for distributing her people to Lance, and he approved it. "I had a word with the yacht club kitchen and crossed a few palms with silver. Your crew can have dinner and breakfast in their dining room. Tell them not to be noisy. They must be perfect ladies and gentlemen. Also tell them: no screwing on the deck of your motor yacht. Confine that activity to their bunks."

"Yes, sir," Betty said, then left.

"That's pretty liberal of you, Lance," Stone said.

"There's no keeping them out of each other's pants," Lance replied. "The best we can do is to keep them out of sight."

The phone rang, and Stone answered.

"It's Dino."

"Hey, there."

"I can shake loose for a few days. Tomorrow morning okay?"

"Sure, and you'll have plenty of company."

"What are you talking about?"

Stone explained the incident of the night before and the presence of the class from the Farm.

"Jesus," Dino said. "I'll be lucky if they don't shoot me."

"Just wear your badge when you're outdoors."

"Sounds like I ought to wear body armor."

"Suit yourself."

21

They had dinner, then Stone took Jenna's seat by the fireplace and moved her to the sofa.

Lance seemed amused. "You're sitting in front of the picture window, deliberately well lit?"

"I do so on your advice," Stone replied.

"On **my** advice?"

"You told me that the new glass is thicker than the old glass, right?"

"Right, but we have not subjected the new glass to the same stresses as the old glass. Nor have we subjected it to any testing."

"That's what we're doing now," Stone said. "We have lots of young people watching the harbor area and the house, do we not?"

"We do."

"Then if there's a shot fired out there, we have a shot at a shot, do we not?"

"This is not the way we normally test equipment."

"Lance, we don't have time to conduct the usual Agency test program, do we?"

"We do not. Nevertheless . . ."

As if in reply to Stone, a series of a half dozen loud noises was heard. Everybody ducked, except Stone, who got up, walked to the window, and began examining the glass. At the same time, from outdoors, weapons were heard firing, and then the roar of an engine reached them, growing less by the second.

"Lance," Stone said, "may I borrow that tiny flashlight in your pocket?"

Lance handed it over, and together, they walked out onto the front porch, and Stone shone the beam on the picture window.

"There," Lance said, pointing. "See the grouping of little smudges?"

Stone lit the area, then rubbed at the glass with a handkerchief from his pocket. The glass rubbed clean, and Stone turned the flashlight on the linen.

"Copper smudges," Lance said. "Full metal jacket."

"My new glass wasn't even scratched. Very effective," Stone said.

"It occurs to me that they could have used mercury-tipped explosive cartridges," Lance said.

"With what effect?" Stone asked.

"Very likely, none."

"I'll keep the new glass," Stone said.

"Your testing methods are very effective, if risky. You must come down to the Farm soon and try out some new equipment for us."

"No, thanks," Stone said.

————

Betty Black walked up out of the trees. "We scored some hits on a boat," she said. "I hope to God it wasn't a fisherman."

"A fisherman with armor-piercing weapons?"

"Did he pierce anything?" she asked.

"Have a look at the window," Lance said, pointing at the spot.

She turned a flashlight onto the glass. "My goodness," she said. "Very effective."

"Did your people hit anybody?"

"Chances are, yes, but we can't prove it. There's a boat out there somewhere with some bullet holes in it, though."

"I should think that would have the effect of discouraging their efforts," Lance said.

"Let's hope so," Stone said. "And tonight, let's put some people in a couple of boats out in the mooring area. If they're foolish enough to try again . . ."

"Anybody dead or mortally wounded out here?" Rawls called from the doorway.

"Maybe," Stone said, "but they're out of our hair."

They went back inside and resumed drinking their cognac.

Stone and Lance met Dino at the airfield the following morning in the station wagon, and they made the next ferry to Lincolnville.

"Where we headed?" Dino asked.

"First, to Camden. And if that's not fruitful, to Rockland," Stone replied. "Lance's people scored some hits on a boat last night, and we want to visit a few boatyards and see if we can find it."

"Good idea."

They drove into Camden Harbor and began trudging from boatyard to boatyard. On the second one they got lucky. There she sat, hauled out and resting on a cradle, a half dozen bullet holes in her transom and a broken pane in the windshield. Her name was **Patsy**.

A foreman strolled over. "Can I help you?" he asked.

"We were looking for that boat," Stone said. "Whose is it?"

"It belonged to a gentleman named Haynes, but he died about a month ago."

"Peacefully?" Stone asked.

"As far as I know."

"How did his boat get so beaten up?"

"Your guess is as good as mine," the man said. "It was stolen the night before last, and she was back in her berth this morning. As you can see, a little worse for the wear. There was an envelope on the front seat with a thousand dollars in cash, but that ain't going to cover it."

"You don't have any idea who took her?"

The man shook his head. "They broke into the office, lifted the keys, then when they brought her back they put everything back the way it was. Except for the bullet holes, I mean. By tomorrow, she'll look the way she always did, and we'll be a few hundred poorer."

Lance took an envelope from his pocket and counted out another thousand. "Will that do it?"

"I guess it will. Did you shoot it up?"

"No, some security guards did that, after somebody aboard this boat put a few rounds into the gentleman's house." He nodded at Stone.

"Anybody hurt?"

"Not at his place. What about on the boat?"

"There was some blood in the cockpit, but we hosed it down this morning."

"If you hadn't done that, we might have known by tonight who stole the boat. Remember, the police like blood."

"Sorry, I didn't think of that. The boat's for sale. I just wanted to get her back on the market as soon as I could. The family could use the money."

"Well, since you failed to secure the boat, give the money to them and file an insurance claim on the yard's policy," Lance said.

"I reckon we can do that."

"Then good morning to you," Lance said, and they walked back to the station wagon.

"Well, I'm glad your kids nicked somebody," Stone said.

Lance snorted. "I wish they'd found brains instead of blood. Then we'd just have to look for somebody with a hole in his head."

"Let's check the ER's," Stone said.

They did so, and a nurse took a look at the admissions log for the night before. "Man with a leg wound," she said. "An accident with a farm implement."

"At 12:34 AM?" Stone asked. "What was he farming, bats?"

"It was a gunshot wound," Lance said. "Did you call the police?"

"No, the attending must have thought it was a plausible story."

"What was the wounded man's name?"

She went back to the computer. "Horace Quinn," she said.

"Close enough to Harley Quince," Stone said. "What address?"

"Green Hills Farm, on Route One," she said.

Lance googled it. "Nothing," he said. "Let's go home, but on the way look for a cowboy hat with a limp."

———

They saw no limping cowboy hats. Mary had crab stew waiting for them, and they gobbled it up.

Betty Black knocked on the rear door and was admitted. "A couple of my people said they're sure they hit somebody."

"At least one of them did," Lance said. "But it was a dead end. It appears to have been Harley Quince. You've got his description. Next time, aim a little higher up; you only nicked a leg."

"I'll issue instructions," she said, then left.

"I wonder if anybody got laid last night," Lance said. "That might account for the near miss."

Rawls came over and received the news. "I know that boat, **Patsy**," he said. "Fella's dead."

"That's what we were told," Stone said. "**Patsy** took half a dozen rounds, though, before they dumped her."

"Any luck finding the wounded guy?"

"He dutifully reported to the ER, gave a false

name and address, got fixed up, and got out," Lance said.

"Ed," Stone said, "was anybody around your place last night?"

"I heard a boat, of a size like **Patsy**, I guess. But it didn't stop, and nobody shot at me."

"Maybe you're next," Stone said. "I don't think they'll come back here tonight, after last night's reception."

"I'll tell Betty to send half of her people over to you, Ed," Lance said. "Be nice to them."

"I'll try not to shoot any of 'em," Ed said.

Harley Quince sat in an easy chair in a hotel room in Rockland with his leg propped up on an ottoman. He got out a throwaway cell phone and dialed the number of another throwaway cell phone in area code 202.

"I can't talk," a male voice said.

"Can you listen?"

"Not long."

"Here's where we are: I stole a boat the other night and got close in to the house, like before, and put half a dozen rounds through that window, except they didn't go through. It was different glass than before, much tougher. I was using armor-piercing ammo."

"Yes?"

"Yes. I took a round in a leg, and it needed

treatment. I used a phony name in the ER. I can hobble around, but only that. I'm going to need a day or two before I can move fast enough to work. Got that?"

"I don't like it, but I got it."

"There's nobody I can trust to do this, so we'll just have to wait. I'll call you back when I've got a plan."

"Okay, bye." He hung up.

Harley took another opioid and lay back and napped.

———

"Wallace? Are you all right? You're red as a beet!"

"Thank you, Senator"—he couldn't remember the man's name—"I'm just fine."

"If you say so," the man said, then walked across the Senate cloakroom and went to his seat. The quorum call bell rang, and Slade went that way, too, swearing under his breath, and taking deep breaths to get his blood pressure down. It didn't work.

———

Ed Rawls sat on his front porch in a cushioned chair and regarded the fresh faces that sat, cross-legged, on the floor. God, he thought, was I ever that young?

"Mr. Rawls," one of them said.

"Call me Ed. I'll call you dummy."

"I don't think it's such a good idea for you to position yourself between us and them. I mean, we've got automatic weapons here."

"You're not supposed to shoot **me**, dummy," Ed growled. "I'm going to be lying on my belly in my boat over there, and when my head pops up, you damn sure better be aiming elsewhere."

"Why don't you give us a clear field of fire, and let us take them out?"

"Can you remember as far back as last night, dummy?"

"Yes, sir, of course."

"You had a clear field of fire, didn't you?"

"Yes, sir."

"And what did you hit?"

"A boat. Several times."

"And yet, the guy driving the boat was okay to visit an ER and get himself some stitches, antibiotics, and painkillers. Did you forget that he was supposed to be too dead to care about that?"

"It was dark."

"That's why you've been issued night goggles, dummy. They didn't think to do that last night, but then I wasn't running the show last night. Tonight will be another story, and **you will not miss!**"

"No, sir."

"Look around you, son. Do you see any cover for you between here and my boat?"

"No, sir."

"That means, by firing from my boat, I'll be fifty yards closer to the target than you will. Are you beginning to get the picture?"

"Yes, sir."

"Well, I'm not entirely certain you are, but if you can just remember not to shoot me, I'll be content. I am one sensational shot, but I don't shoot well when my hair has been recently parted."

"No, sir."

"Okay, let's run through it again."

"Yes, sir."

They ran through it again.

24

Lance accepted a drink from Stone. "Thank you. Do you mind if I use Dick's secret office for a while?"

"Feel free."

"What's the best hotel in Rockland?"

Stone went into the living room and got a brochure naming the dozen best Rockland hotels. "Take your pick," he said.

Lance dialed the first number, and it was promptly answered by a young woman. "Would you connect me with your guest, Mr. Harley Quince?" he asked.

"One moment, please," she replied.

There was a **click**, and a man said, "Yeah?"

Lance wanted to hang up immediately. He hadn't expected to find Quince so quickly, and he didn't have a plan. "I beg your pardon," he said, slipping into full Brit mode. "I believe I may have been put through to a wrong number. Please forgive me." He hung up and walked into the living room. "I've found Harley Quince," he said.

"Where?" Stone asked.

"At the Rockland Harbor Hotel."

"On that list I gave you?"

"Number one on that list. I called, he answered, I gave him the British version of 'Sorry, wrong number,' and hung up."

"What did he say?"

"He said, 'Yeah.'"

"What do we do now?" Dino asked.

"I don't quite know," Lance said. "We're not the police, we don't have a warrant, and the last ferry has sailed."

"We could call the state police, Sergeant Young," Stone said.

"And tell him what?"

"Ask him to get a warrant?"

"On what evidence?"

"A bullet in the leg?"

"An **alleged** bullet in the leg. He has a leg wound, but we can't prove it's from a bullet. The ER doctor bought his story, or he would have called the police."

"Is there some way we could do this, ah, extra-legally?" Stone asked.

"You mean, send a sniper over there and shoot him?"

"I'd like to point out that I didn't say that," Stone said.

"How about charging him with stealing the boat?" Dino asked.

"He returned the boat and left a thousand dollars on the seat. He would say he rented it."

"But the boat is full of bullet holes."

"Not anymore."

"We'd have the boatyard manager's testimony."

"What could he testify to? He never saw Quince."

"He could testify to the . . . former holes," Stone said.

"The renter damaged the boat, he paid for the damage."

"How about attempted murder?"

"Who's the attemptee?"

"I am," Stone said.

"Then why aren't you dead? Can you otherwise prove you were shot at?"

"We all heard the gunshots."

"We heard a noise, and there's not a mark on the glass."

"Why are you making this difficult, Lance?"

"I'm not making it difficult. I'm trying to make it possible. All we've got on our side is a bunch of armed kids, who have fired their weapons, which is against Maine law, unless you've got a hunting license."

"Maybe Ed Rawls will get a shot at him tonight?"

"Quince's not going anywhere tonight. He's wounded."

They had another drink and sat around, disconsolately. Finally, one by one, they went to bed.

———

Ed Rawls lay on the floorboards of his boat for two hours, then he said to himself, "Quince's not coming. He's wounded." He grabbed his baseball cap, stuck it on a burgee staff, and raised it above the level of the gunwales. He heard a **pfft** noise, and the cap flew away.

"Hold your goddamned fire!" he yelled.

"Sorry, Mr. Rawls," a young woman's voice said.

"I'm standing up now. Don't fucking kill me!" he shouted.

"Yes, sir. I mean, no, sir."

Rawls stood up and survived. "All right," he said to the night air, "he ain't going to show. Let's pack it in and get some sleep."

Shadowy figures moved out of the bushes and filed off toward the barn.

Ed watched them go, then went into the house and found his throwaway phone.

"Hello," Stone said sleepily.

"Quince's not going to show," Ed said.

"He's wounded."

"Well, we're gonna get some sleep."

"We did that an hour ago," Stone said, then hung up.

"Sorry to wake you," Ed said to the dial tone.

25

Senator Wallace Slade, Republican of Texas, leaned into the wind and tugged on the brim of his Stetson. A tumbleweed sped by, followed by a cloud of dust. Slade reined in his horse, held a palm up to his hat brim, and stared into the distance. Another puff of dust blew by, and cattle lowed off camera.

"Cut!" someone yelled. "Good for me. Good for you, Senator?"

"Shit, yes," the senator grumbled.

"Okay, strike it. We're wrapped on this location. Let's move it onto the soundstage!"

Someone shut off the wind machine. Someone else dragged a platform up to the horse, so the rider could dismount without pulling a muscle, which he did, and the horse was led away, following a large carrot held in front of him.

"We'll be ready for you first thing tomorrow," the director of the campaign commercial said to Slade. "Eleven AM."

A script girl materialized, clutching a glass of a single-malt Scotch, which Slade relieved her of, then he got into the rear seat of the Bentley and was driven off to his borrowed bungalow to change into his tux for dinner. The Scotch had evaporated by the time he got to the front door.

A young man waited for him in the sitting room, clutching a half dozen storyboards. "You want to see the updates for today, sir?" he asked.

"Get me another Scotch," Slade said, tossing him the heavy whisky glass. He got out of his clothes, sank into an easy chair, and accepted the drink while still in his underwear. The phone rang. "What's happening?" he asked.

"How are you, Senator?"

"I've just driven a herd of cattle from Plainview to Wichita. How would you feel?"

"Bushed, I guess."

Slade pulled on the Scotch. "What's happening? Don't make me ask you again."

"Not a whole lot. I put half a dozen armor-piercing rounds through Barrington's front window. I had Jenna zeroed in, but the glass was more than I figured on. Then we came under fire from half a dozen guns and had to beat it out of there and back to Camden. There was three grands' damage to the boat we, ah, borrowed. I had to pay cash, so I'll send you the bill."

"Well, shit."

"And on top of that, I took a bullet, had to go to the hospital. Don't worry, I used another name and address."

"A bullet, where? In the ass?"

"Sort of. They sutured the wound, but I'm not going to be able to walk right for a few days. They've got me on crutches."

"Can you find me another shooter by tomorrow?"

"That would be tough, sir, but I'll be able to go in a couple of days. Right now, they're ready for us. We need the element of surprise in our favor. So I suggest we let it cool down before we take another shot. Anyway, she's already testified, right? She can't hurt us no more."

"She can hurt us as long as she can walk around and talk. I'm depending on you to see that she can't do either one. Now you get this done in quick time, or I'm going to put somebody on **your** ass." Slade slammed down the phone and drained his glass.

A woman came out of the bedroom. "Your tux is on the bed, Senator. And Costumes sent over the full kit—shirt, shoes, vest, and bow tie. Do you want me to stick around and tie it for you?"

"I'll manage," Slade said. "Get out. And tell that boy to bring me another Scotch."

"Yes, sir."

———

She left by the front door, and the boy was waiting with a bottle of Scotch. "He wants another," she said. "Have you got any cyanide handy? He could use a little of that for a chaser."

The boy snickered. "I wish," he said.

26

Stone was reading a book before the fireplace in the early afternoon when the doorbell rang, baffling him. Who could be ringing the doorbell? Nobody knew they were there. He got up, took the handgun from his belt, racked the slide, putting a round up the spout, cocked it, put the safety on, then returned it to his gun belt.

He walked to the front door, peered through the peephole, and found a man, dressed in a suit, his back to the door. Stone drew his handgun and opened the door, concealing his weapon behind it. "Yes?" he said.

The man looked over his shoulder. "Are you Barrington?"

"Who's asking?"

"Bob Burnham."

"State your business."

"I have an appointment."

"Not with me, you don't."

"With Jenna Jacoby."

"Stay there," Stone said, and closed the door. He picked up the house phone and paged Jenna.

"Yes?"

"There's a man here, sounds like a Texan, named Bob Burnham, says he has an appointment with you."

"Oh, yes. He's my congressman. Please let him in."

"A Texas congressman is making house calls in Maine?"

"I asked him to come."

Stone opened the front door. "I'm going to have to frisk you, Congressman," he said.

"I'm unarmed." He spread his legs and his arms, and Stone felt him up and down. "All right, come in." He pointed the man at the sofa before the fireplace. "Take a seat over there, and don't move around."

The man sat. "Is it too early for a drink?" he asked.

"Yes. We don't do business until after five."

Jenna came down the stairs and Burnham rose to meet her. She shook his hand, but no kiss, then she sat down in the chair opposite Stone. "What can I do for you?"

"It may sound odd, but I'm looking for a campaign contribution."

"In Maine?" she asked.

"Let me explain."

"Please do," she said.

"Your husband . . ."

"Are you referring to my ex-husband?"

"I'm sorry, I didn't know it was final."

"Go on."

"I'm your congressman, and I'm primarying Senator Slade." He got no reaction. "I'm running against him for his Senate seat in the Republican primary."

"And do you have any sort of chance?"

"I don't know if you've been out of touch, but there was an incident widely reported in the media, of his having lunch in the House of Lords dining room, in London, while wearing his hat."

"That came to my attention," she said.

"Well, we've been tracking the polls very carefully, and to our surprise, that occasion caused a seven-point downturn in his job-approval rating among likely voters in the primary."

"I'm delighted to hear it," Jenna said.

"I'm here to encourage that trend," Burnham said. "I'm announcing tomorrow that I'm running against him for the seat."

Everybody was silent for a moment.

"How's **your** job-approval rating?" Stone asked.

"Up seven points."

"I can see how you might be encouraged," Jenna said. "How can I help?"

"By giving a large contribution to my campaign and letting me announce it tomorrow."

Jenna burst out laughing. "Well, good luck to you! How much do you want?"

"A thousand dollars," he said. "Preferably in a check with your name printed on it."

"I can do that," Jenna said. She got up, found her purse, and began rummaging in it. "I even have a nice Mont Blanc fountain pen with which to write it." She opened her checkbook.

"Just make it out to 'Burnham for Senate,'" he said.

She wrote the check, waved it around, then blew on it and handed it over.

"Perfect," he said, gazing at it.

"Anything else?"

"Perhaps a statement?"

"What sort of statement?"

"Unkind. Inflammatory, if you like. I'll read it after I've shown your check at my announcement."

Jenna found a pad, thought a little, then wrote a few words. "How's this? 'I heartily endorse the election of Bob Burnham to the United States Senate, a seat currently held by my former husband, Wallace Slade, whose grip is slipping in more ways than one.'"

"Perfection," Burnham said.

She handed him the sheet, and he politely made his goodbyes and started for the door.

"Excuse me, Congressman," Stone said. "May I ask how you found us here?"

"I got off the ferry and made the first right," Burnham replied.

"No, I mean, how did you know Ms. Jacoby was here? And how did you know where to look for her?"

"Oh. Her sister, Jamie, told me. I met her in Camden yesterday."

"Thank you," Stone said. "If you hurry, you can just make the return ferry."

Burnham hurried.

Stone closed and locked the door behind him.

"Well," Jenna said. "That was the most fun I've ever had for a thousand dollars."

"Jenna," Stone said. "What is your sister doing in Camden?"

"Shopping, I should think. She'll get a later ferry."

"You invited her here?"

"Well, yes. There's plenty of room, isn't there? She can share my room."

"Had you planned to mention this to me?"

"I guess it slipped my mind."

"The last person your sister sent to my door tried to shoot both you and me. Do you recall that?"

"That was an accident. I didn't know that a cell phone could be traced."

"Was it an accident that she sent a stranger to my door?"

"She knew who he was."

"Oh? Had they ever met? Or could he have been one of Wallace's thugs, misrepresenting himself to her?"

"Jamie has very good judgment about people," Jenna said. "Now, if my sister is not welcome here, I'll hitch a ride with her to the ferry."

"And then what? Or where?"

"Wherever I fucking well like," Jenna said.

Stone got out his phone and pressed a button. "Jenna is leaving my house with her sister in an hour or two. She'll be on the four o'clock ferry if you want to put security on her." He hung up without waiting for a reply.

"Perhaps you had better go and pack," Stone said. "Just ask Seth to put your luggage into your sister's car."

He sat back, opened his book, and began to read again, while Jenna stomped up the stairs.

27

Seth came into the living room. "Miz Jacoby asked me to come get her luggage and put it into her sister's car, when she gets here."

"Please do as she asks, Seth."

"Do you want me to ride shotgun?"

"No. Apparently, Ms. Jacoby feels that she is perfectly safe now."

"Okay." Seth started up the stairs and nearly ran into Jenna, who was on the way down.

"You all packed, ma'am?" Seth asked.

"No, Seth. I won't be going." She went and sat by the fireplace with Stone. "I've told my sister I won't be going with her," she said.

"And how did you communicate that to her?"

"I called her on . . ." She stopped.

"Your cell phone?"

"I'm sorry, yes."

"Seth," Stone said. "Would you please go to the village store and buy two throwaway cell phones? Put them on my account."

"Yes, sir." Seth left.

Nothing was said for a while. Finally, Jenna said, "What's a throwaway cell phone?"

"It's self-defined," Stone replied. "Each one has its own number. When you call your sister or anyone else, they see an unidentified number. When you're finished with it, you throw it away."

Seth was back in a minute with a paper bag. "Give them to Ms. Jacoby, please." He did so.

"Now," Stone said to Jenna. "You plug them in to charge, and after a couple of hours, they're ready to use. Give me your old phone, please."

She handed it over.

Stone removed the SIM card and returned the phone to her. "This won't work anymore. When you get back to wherever, you can get a new SIM card and number, or just trade in your phone for the new model."

"I can't make calls now?"

Stone pointed. "Sit in that chair and plug a phone into the wall, then you can use it while it charges. Use the other as a backup."

"I was inconsiderate. I'm sorry."

"All right."

"That wasn't a very forgiving response."

"It wasn't much of an apology."

The doorbell rang.

"I expect that will be your sister, but use the peephole before you unlock the door."

Jenna went to the front door, checked the peephole, and let in her sister.

"Lock the door," Stone said.

She did so. "I'm sorry. This is my sister, Jamie Jacoby. Jamie, this is my host, Stone Barrington." The two resembled each other strongly, almost like twins.

"How do you do?" Stone said, half rising.

"I do pretty good," Jamie said. "Jenna, are you ready? Where's your luggage?"

"I've decided not to go, Jamie."

"Why not?"

"Because Stone feels that I'm still in danger and leaving this house would put both you and me in jeopardy."

"Nobody's trying to kill me," Jamie said.

"It would be very easy for you to become collateral damage," Stone said.

"How?"

"If someone makes an attempt on Jenna, you could both be killed. Jenna has already withstood two attempts on her life, after she was tracked to this house when she used her cell phone to call you."

Jenna wrote down the throwaway's number and handed it to her. "Use this number if you want to reach me. My old number doesn't work anymore."

"Why doesn't it work?"

"Because I disabled it," Stone said. "And don't use your own phone, please, until you're off the island."

"Jamie," Jenna said. "Let's go sit on the back porch until it's time for your ferry. We'll have some iced tea." She took her sister by the elbow and propelled her out the door. Stone called Mary and asked for the tea to be taken out to them. He could see from their animation that they were arguing about Jenna's decision. Their tea arrived, and their discussion continued. Finally, Jamie set down her glass and walked through the living room to the front door. Stone let her out and locked the door behind her.

"Does she understand now?" Stone asked.

"Not really. Jamie believes that events occur on her own schedule."

"I hope she's correct—at least, until she's back on the mainland."

They heard the car start and spew gravel on the way out. A few seconds later, as Stone and Jenna watched, Jamie's car exploded.

———

Another two minutes passed until Ed Rawls arrived. Stone was outside near the car, holding a shotgun.

"What the fuck?" Rawls asked.

"It's Jenna's sister." Stone nodded toward her car.

"Did you call nine-one-one?"

"Of course," Stone replied.

"How did this happen?"

"Jamie, her name was, preferred to make her own security arrangements—that is, none to speak of. She had been intending to take Jenna with her off the island."

"Well," Rawls said, "she's gonna miss the ferry."

28

Jenna tried to run to the car, but Stone held her back. "You can't help Jamie," he said. "She's gone." He got her back inside, with Ed's help, and seated her on the sofa.

Stone poured her some bourbon, and she gulped half of it. "Try and be calm, Jenna," he said. "Do you want to go upstairs and lie down until the authorities get here?"

"That will be some time," Rawls said. "They'll either have to take the ferry or fly in."

"There are two already on the island," Stone said.

"Jamie never hurt anybody," Jenna said. "Look," she said, pointing. "She left her handbag. She was always doing that. All she was trying to do was help me."

Ed poured himself a drink and sat down in the chair across from her. "Do you think Jamie would still help you, if she could?"

Jenna took a Kleenex from the box on the coffee table and blew her nose. "Of course she would, if she could."

Rawls picked up Jamie's handbag, looked inside, and removed a .380 semiautomatic pistol from it and set it on the table, then he examined the other contents. "The usual ID," he said, holding up a wallet and looking at the driver's license. "The two of you look very much alike."

Stone caught Ed's drift. "Jenna, do you think Jamie would step into your shoes for a while, if she could?"

"Yes, she would. No doubt about it."

"Then why don't we let her do that?"

Jenna looked sharply at Stone. "What do you mean?"

Stone nodded at the front door. "That could have been you in the car. Does it belong to her?"

"No, it's a rental. She was going to turn it in at Bangor airport before her flight."

Ed went into the handbag again and found an airline ticket.

"The police will be here soon. I think it would be a good idea if you go upstairs and lie down while they're here. I'll tell them you're too upset to talk to them now, that you'll phone them later, when they're back at their offices. You go be Jamie for a while."

Jenna got it. "Do you think that would work?"

"No one can kill a person who's already dead," Ed said.

"It's the safest possible solution," Stone said. "We can sort it all out later, when this is over."

"I think I would like to go upstairs and rest for a while," Jenna said, standing.

"An excellent idea," Ed said.

She took the Kleenex box and walked slowly up the stairs.

As she did, a helicopter flew in and hovered over the house and the smoking remains of the car for a moment or two, then flew off toward the airstrip.

Seth had been silently standing by.

"You understand about the names?" Stone asked Seth.

"Yes, sir. I'll tell them Miss Jamie is resting upstairs." He left to get the station wagon.

"Ed," Stone said, "put everything back in the bag except the pistol and any ammunition."

Ed saw to that and handed the weapon to Stone, who took it into Dick Stone's office and put it into a drawer. The doorbell rang.

Stone greeted the two Maine State Police officers who lived on the island. "Sergeant Young, I believe the problem is obvious."

"So, your worst fears have been realized?"

"Yes, they have."

The sergeant nodded, and the two men walked carefully around the smoking hulk of the car and viewed the remains inside.

"The ME is on the chopper," he said. "You said you saved that piece of glass that stopped a bullet the other night?"

"Over here," Stone said, taking him over to where the damaged pane rested against the garage.

"That's heavy-duty stuff, isn't it?" the sergeant said.

"The replacement is even more impressive."

"Do you think I could clear your MG out of the garage? The ME is going to need a place to do his preliminary examination."

"Certainly," Stone said, handing him the keys.

"I understand there's a sister here."

"Yes, she's upstairs resting. She took a sedative, I think. You won't be able to question her today, but I can have her call you tomorrow morning."

"That'll do," Young replied, and went to move the MG, just as Seth returned from the airfield with the ME and his assistant.

————

They sat in the living room and sipped iced tea and ate some of Mary's chocolate-chip cookies.

"Well," the ME said, "time of death: four-forty-five PM, according to testimony and the stopped clock in the car. This date. Cause of death: explosion and fire. She died instantly from the shock."

"We'll remove the wreckage to our shop at base," Young said. "And our explosives people will make their determination there. A truck with a crane is on the next ferry."

As if on cue, a large truck pulled into the driveway.

"I've photographed her driver's license," Young said, laying it on the table. "It squares with her passport in her bag. J. B. Jacoby."

They stood up. "We'll load the wreckage and be on our way," Young said. "I'll get the ME back to the chopper."

Stone showed them out and came back to the living room, where Rawls was pouring them a drink.

"Close enough on the name," he said. "I think they bought it all."

"That's a relief. I think you can ship all those kids back to the Farm. Don't tell them anything but the cover story."

Lance knocked on the door and let himself in. "I take it all is well."

"As well as can be," Stone said.

"I'll see that the story is circulated in the right places," he said. "The media will be calling the senator today for comment."

"What better way to announce it?" Stone said.

29

Stone read the papers over breakfast. The **International New York Times** had the most concise report:

SENATOR'S EX-WIFE MURDERED

Jenna B. Jacoby, who was recently divorced from Senator Wallace Slade (R-Tex), was killed in the explosion and subsequent fire of her rental car on an island in Penobscot Bay, Maine, yesterday, while en route from the home of a friend to Bangor airport, from where she had planned to fly to New York.

Ms. Jacoby, whose maiden name was restored in the divorce, was a top model in

New York City during the early part of this century. She had been the subject of at least three attempts on her life prior to her testimony to a joint committee of Congress, where she testified to the character and criminal activity of Senator Slade, calling him, among other things, "a thief and a murderer."

The Maine State Police are investigating and have described Senator Slade as a "person of interest."

Jenna came downstairs slowly and, over breakfast, was shown the **Times.** "Well," she said, "I'm glad they got in 'thief and a murderer.'"

"It's the least he deserved," Stone said. "How are you feeling?"

"Sad about Jamie," she said, "but happy to be alive."

"The Gulfstream is picking us up at Rockland. We'll leave for the airfield here in half an hour. Are you all packed?"

"Yes, I'm all set," she said.

"You'll be safe at my house in New York," Stone said. "You can make plans from there."

She held up a strand of hair. "I've got to shorten this, to look more like Jamie. I'll need different makeup, too."

"I have someone who will come to the house for that."

"How long before I can shop openly in New York?"

"A few days, I think."

"I miss shopping."

After they landed back home in New York, Stone was in his office with Jenna when Joan buzzed. "Two gentlemen from the FBI to see you."

"Send them to the study. Jenna, you stay here. We'll call you if they want to talk to you." He went upstairs to meet them. Stone introduced himself.

"Actually, we're here to see Ms. Jacoby," one of them said.

"On what business? I'm her attorney."

"You're aware, then, that killing a federal employee is a federal crime?"

"Yes, but . . ."

"Ms. Jacoby was carried on the books of Senator Slade's Senate office as an assistant press secretary."

"I'm not aware. Why don't we ask her?" He called Joan and asked her to bring "Jamie" upstairs.

Jenna shook the men's hands and sat down.

"Our condolences on the death of Jenna," one of them said.

"Thank you."

"Ms. Jacoby, are you aware that your sister was

listed on Senator Slade's staff list as an assistant press secretary?"

"No, I was not, but it would be just like Wallace to list her as such, then pocket her salary."

"Nevertheless, she qualifies as a federal employee, making her murder a federal crime."

"I'm delighted to hear it," Jenna said. "I'm sure you have much greater resources at hand than the Maine police."

"You were the last person she talked with at any length," the agent said. "Can you tell us what you talked about?"

"Wallace and his attempts on her life, mostly. Also, about Harley Quince."

"Who is that?" the agent asked, taking notes.

"He is, to put it bluntly, an assassin and enforcer for Wallace Slade."

"We'll look into him."

"We know him to have been on the island for several days," Stone said. "He tried to shoot Jenna in my living room, but his rifle bullet ran into armored glass." He explained why the windows were armored.

"Do you know his whereabouts now?"

"Well, his work is done, so I expect he will have left the island."

"For where?"

"For wherever Wallace Slade is," Jenna said. "They're never far apart."

"On the day of Jenna's murder," the agent

said, "Senator Slade was in Texas, filming a campaign commercial and attending a black-tie
fundraiser that evening."

"He would arrange to be elsewhere, wouldn't
he?" Stone asked. "You can place Harley Quince
at a Rockland Harbor Hotel, possibly under the
name of Horace Quinn, which is the name
he gave the emergency room where he was treated
for a bullet wound in the leg. I would call that an
identifying mark."

"Who gave him a bullet wound?"

"We had security for the house, and his fire
was returned." Stone told them about the boat,
Patsy, and everything else he knew.

"During all this time, did you talk to anyone
in law enforcement?"

Stone gave him the name of Sergeant Young of
the Maine police. "Oh, and the police commissioner of New York City, who was my houseguest
in Maine."

"That's pretty good law enforcement."

They started to ask more questions, but Stone
held up a hand. "Jamie, will you excuse us for a
little while?"

"Of course," she said, and left the room.

"Mr. Barrington," an agent said, "we're here to
talk to Ms. Jacoby, not you."

"Well, I'm all you're going to get," Stone said,
"and I'll tell you why."

30

The agent leaned forward and took a deep breath.

"Hold it right there," Stone said. "My client does not wish to speak to you further, but I do."

"All right, go ahead."

"First, I'm going to have to ask you both for your promise that you will not tell anyone except your AIC at the Bureau what I'm going to say."

They exchanged a puzzled look.

"It's necessary for the health and safety of my client."

"Oh, all right," one said, and the other nodded.

"I'm aware that it is a felony to lie to a federal agent, and that's why I asked my client to leave: she would have been required to lie to you."

"Could you try to make a little more sense?" one agent asked.

"My client is Jenna Jacoby."

"The dead sister?"

"No, the other sister, Jamie, was the one killed in the car explosion. My client is Jenna, who you just met."

"I think I'm beginning to get this," the agent said.

"Great," his partner replied, "you can explain it to me."

"Jenna was being hunted like an animal," Stone said. "With the death of her sister, we had an opportunity to keep her alive without a platoon of security guards. If Wallace Slade and his minion, Harley Quince, believe Jenna is dead, then they'll stop trying to kill her."

"Ahhh," both agents said. "So, all we have to do to help is lie to our AIC?"

"Certainly not, just swear him to secrecy."

"We can't swear that he'll buy that."

"Then if he doesn't buy it and Jenna is killed because of that, ask him how he'd like a monumental civil suit against the Bureau for causing her death."

"I don't think he'd like that very much."

"Good, then we're all on the same page," Stone said.

———

Stone showed them out and went back to his desk and buzzed Joan. "Ask Jenna to come in again, please."

She came in and sat down.

"I'm sorry, I had to ask you to leave so that you wouldn't tell them the lie I asked you to tell them."

"Oh, really?"

"It's against the law to lie to an FBI agent. Instead, I swore them to secrecy and asked them to swear their boss to secrecy, too."

"And you think that'll work?"

"Maybe. At least it will give us some time to figure out what to do with you next. Do you just want to hole up here? That's fine with me, but maybe you've thought of someplace you'd rather be."

"It's getting chilly out. I'd rather be someplace warmer for the winter."

"How about Key West?" Stone asked. "I have a house there, and there are firearms in the safe."

"Sold," she said.

Joan came into his office. "Jenna's hairdresser and makeup artist is here."

"Go get bobbed," Stone said, and she did.

Stone had some lunch and did some work. Jenna returned a couple of hours later.

"Wow!" Stone said.

"You like? We used the passport photo. Jamie wore glasses, too. I can take out my contacts."

"I don't think you'll need to," Stone said.

"The change to summer clothes will help, too. I'll do some shopping when I get there."

"When do you want to go?"

"I'll need to stock up on the sexual experience for a couple of days," she said.

"I think we can arrange that."

"Then book me a ticket."

Stone buzzed Joan and gave her instructions.

Jenna went upstairs for a nap, and Joan buzzed again. "There's a Mr. Quince to see you," she said. "He doesn't have an appointment."

"See that Jenna doesn't come down while he's here, and send him in."

Quince walked into the office, and Joan snuck up behind him and snatched his hat off. "I'll keep this for you," she said, and slammed the door before he could object.

"What can I do for you, Mr. Quince?" Stone asked. He didn't sit down and didn't offer him a seat. "I don't have much time."

"Maybe you'd have more time for my boss," Quince said.

"And who's that?"

"Senator Wallace Slade."

"No, not for him, either. What do you want?"

"The senator wants to hire you."

"For what?"

"For a lawyer."

"I'm not available to Mr. Slade."

"You mean **Senator** Slade."

"'Mister' is a perfectly respectful form of address, even for a senator."

"Make yourself available."

"What sort of legal work does Slade want done?"

"He's being stalked by a woman."

"Tell him to call the police. We have a very good anti-stalking law in this state."

"He'd rather keep it private."

"Then tell him to hire a private detective."

"He don't know any private dicks."

"Tell him to try Google. Now, I'm all out of time. Good day." Stone sat down and started to read a document, but Quince didn't move. Stone looked up. "Why are you still here?"

"I'm trying to think of how I can persuade my boss not to kill you," Quince said.

"He's already tried," Stone said, "and it didn't work. I'm not as easy to kill as Jenna Jacoby, and I can counterpunch."

"Jenna's death was a tragic accident," Quince said.

"Tragic, yes. Nothing accidental about it. Now that it occurs to me, the Maine State Police would like to have a word with you."

"I got nothing to say to them."

"Well, when they find you, they'll think of something. I can tip them off as to your whereabouts." He buzzed Joan three times.

Joan came into the office with Quince's hat in

one hand and her .45 in the other. She slapped his hat into his belly. "This way out," shesaid.

"If you have to shoot him," Stone said, "go for a head shot."

"Love to," Joan replied. Quince brushed past her and left.

"The .45 was a nice touch," Stone said.

"I thought so, too." Joan went back to her desk. Then Stone heard her locking the front door.

31

Stone called Lance. "Scrambled."

"Me, too," Lance said. "What's up?"

"We've got problems with Jenna."

"So, solve them."

"Not so easily done. And they have to be solved now, or they'll cause a whole new set of problems."

"All right," Lance said wearily. "Tell me about it."

"At the moment, Jenna is Jamie, because you and I and she say she is. No other reason."

"Why is that a problem?"

"Jenna is a wealthy woman, but she can't write a check, can't use a credit card, can't speak to her investment advisers, none of that."

"I see your point," Lance said. "So, how do we fix that?"

"We would have to make the change from Jenna to Jamie permanent."

"But?"

"That would cause, I think, even more problems. If we take the usual steps for declaring somebody dead, we need official documents, like a death certificate, and putting a false name on one of those is a criminal act. In fact, in the future, almost any action she might take of a financial or documentary nature would be criminal."

"So, what do we do?"

"That was my next question to you. I'm hoping you'll have some rational and legal suggestions."

"What are you saying?"

"I'm saying I don't know what the fuck we're going to do. Now, do you want to take a stab at this?"

Lance emitted a long and deep sigh. "No, I don't."

"I can think of one thing that might work, but it has dangers."

"Please, please tell me."

"Jenna goes back to being Jenna. We announce Jamie is dead. Jenna is Jenna. Then she can do all the things a person needs to do, legally and morally."

"That is nearly an ideal solution," Lance said.

"Yes, nearly."

"You mean except for the part about Slade trying to kill her?"

"That's it, you've got it!"

"And you think that's still a problem?"

"Only moments ago, one Harley Quince turned up at my office to say that Wallace Slade wants me to be his attorney."

"How did you react to that?"

"Unsatisfactorily, from Slade's point of view. Joan ushered Quince out with his hat in his hand and a .45 pressed to his spine."

"What do you suppose Slade had in mind?"

"Access to Jenna's estate, which has a net worth of more than sixty million dollars. The divorce court gave Slade nearly nada."

"So, we can't allow that to happen."

"If it should happen, I would be representing Jenna."

"Can Slade be bought off?"

"With whose money? I wouldn't allow my client to give him a dime, and I can't imagine you doing it with government funds."

"Of course not."

"She's no longer a congressional witness," Stone pointed out.

"No, she's not."

"So, I don't see how you could justify the student population of the Farm sitting around, waiting for something terrible to happen. We've already tried that plan, with the death of her sister as the result."

"Do not ever speak those words to another human being or recording device," Lance said firmly.

"We need a long-range plan."

"We could kill Wallace Slade," Lance said tentatively.

"And Harley Quince and whoever else cheerfully does Slade's bidding? Come on, Lance. You should never speak those words again, not even in American Sign Language. Somebody might see you."

"Has Jenna expressed to you anything regarding her future?"

"She says she'd like to spend the winter in a warm place."

"Did you offer her Key West?"

"That came up."

"Did you agree to it?"

"Sort of."

"Then that's our next step, isn't it?"

"In Key West she could never leave the house or speak to anyone."

"I can live with that," Lance said.

"Perhaps, but Jenna couldn't. She's a . . . social creature, and she needs . . . entertainment, from time to time."

"You mean daily?"

"Perhaps a bit more frequently."

"So, if we lock her in the house and you fuck her twice a day, we'd be fine?"

"Can we take a step back toward reality, please?" Stone asked.

"Is reality an available option?"

"Well, Jenna can afford, say, a four-man or -woman detail from Strategic Services."

"Can you house them in Key West?"

"Just barely. That's not a permanent solution."

"We need that."

"Tell me, Lance, does the Agency have a safe house in a favorable climate? I mean, in this country?"

"I would have to research that."

"Then, Lance, pick up the phone and tell somebody to research it. I don't expect you to pore through the real estate listings in the Sunday **Times**. And West Africa won't do."

Lance sighed again. "I'll get back to you."

"Pleeeeease do."

Stone hung up, nearly panting with the effort of the call.

32

Stone, Jenna, Dino, and Viv were having dinner in the kitchen booth downstairs, talking of not much, when Jenna brought them to attention.

"I have a job," she said.

Everybody else stopped talking. Images flashed through Stone's mind of her in the typing pool at Steele Insurance.

"Tell more," Stone finally managed to say.

"It's a modeling job. A trusted friend booked it for me," Jenna said. "It's the cover of a mother/daughter special edition of **Vogue**." She looked around at the blank faces staring at her. "I'm the mother," she said.

"Oh," Stone said.

"Let me see if I can answer the questions you

probably have," Jenna said. "First of all, it shoots tomorrow, but it doesn't publish for another couple of months."

"Are you getting a published credit for the work?" Viv asked. "I mean, on the contents page where it gives the name of the cover photographer: Does it also give your name?"

"The photographer is Harry Benson."

"Good. Wonderful," Viv said. "Does it give your name?"

"Yes."

"Which name?"

"Jenna Jacoby."

Each of the diners emitted an unintelligible sound.

"I can't go on being Jamie," Jenna said. "Being her means that I don't exist. I tried to use a credit card on a phone purchase today, and they said the card account was closed. I can't go into my bank and cash a check." She looked around the table at their faces. "Is anybody hearing what I'm saying?"

"Actually," Stone said, "I spent half an hour on the phone with Lance Cabot today, explaining that very thing to him."

"And what did Lance say?"

"He said, and I quote: 'I'll get back to you.'"

"Has he?"

"Not yet."

"I can't go on being dead," Jenna said. "I can't live that way."

"Literally, true," Viv said.

"So, what's the answer?"

"The answer to what?" Dino asked.

"We need all the publications that said I was dead to say that I'm not."

"I think the news report that you are not dead would get more media coverage than the one that said you were."

Dino spoke up. "I can see the line on the 'corrections' page in the **Times**: 'Last week we said Jenna Jacoby was dead. She is not. Our apologies to everyone who thought she was.'"

"Do you think they will also say that Senator Wallace Slade, R-Tex, didn't murder her?" Stone asked. "Otherwise, he's going to sue the socks off them."

"That's Lance's problem, isn't it?" Dino asked.

"Yes, but I don't want to be the one telling him that."

"Are you afraid he'll press a button and dissolve the phone in your hand?"

"Something like that," Stone said. "And my ear with it."

"Okay, that's **your** problem."

"Let's go back to the root of this business," Viv said. "Who was the first person to say that Jenna was Jamie?"

"I don't think that anybody actually spoke those words," Stone said. "The idea just sort of descended from above."

"You're blaming God?" Viv asked.

"No, no, it was just so obvious that we all went along with it."

"How did it get into the papers?"

"I don't know. Lance sort of jiggled an elbow or something, and the next thing we knew, it was on the AP wire."

"So, it's Lance's elbow's problem?"

"Sort of."

"Then you'd better add that to the list of other things you have to tell Lance."

"I'll try to remember that. Anybody want dessert?"

———

Stone was at his desk the next morning when Joan buzzed him. "Lance on one."

Stone picked up. "Hello?"

"Scramble."

"I'm scrambled."

"You're sure? I don't want any mistakes about that."

"Is this conversation being recorded?"

"You should assume," Lance said, "that any phone conversation with a high official in American Intelligence is being recorded."

"Okay, I'll listen, but I won't talk."

"Then how can you tell me what I need to know?"

Stone remained silent.

"Stone?"

"I'm listening."

"Oh, all right, I'll turn it off. There. You are not being recorded."

"You swear?"

"You can't ask me to swear. I'm not testifying."

"I don't care, I want you to swear you're not recording this conversation. I want it on the tape."

"I swear this conversation is not being recorded. There, it's on the tape."

"Okay. Jenna is out right now, breaking cover."

"That's an odd locution."

"It's a bird-hunting expression, I think. Possibly quail. I'm not sure about that."

"How is she breaking cover?"

"She's being photographed by Harry Benson for the cover of **Vogue**, as we speak."

"Jesus H. Christ!"

"You read that somewhere."

"Tell me more!"

"It's for a mother/daughter issue. Jenna is the mother. It comes out in a couple of months, and her name will appear on an inside page."

"But she'll look like Jamie, what with the new hair and makeup."

"Who knows? But her cover will be blown."

"Well, at least we'll have some time to get her dead again."

"She won't have it, Lance. She says she's Jenna again, and you have to make everybody who said she was dead take it back."

"That's not a problem. We'll just say that she's alive. That will make nationwide headlines."

"That's good for me," Stone said. "But what are you going to do about the odious Wallace Slade?"

"Do? Why do I have to do?"

"Because your first news story implied that he murdered her, or had it done. He could sue, big-time."

"There is no such news story with my name on it," Lance said resolutely. "I do not do bylines."

"Okay, problem solved. Now, how about the one about keeping Jenna alive?"

"If she's going to 'break cover,' as you so sportingly put it, then she's on her own. I'm having nothing to do with **Vogue**, and I'm having nothing to do with subsequent events, whatever they might be."

"Well," Stone said, "that solves all your problems. I'll explain it to her."

"Don't mention my name," Lance said.

"What?"

"We're recording again, now." He hung up.

33

S tone and Jenna made affectionate love that evening. And when they were exhausted, he took a deep breath and spoke.

"Jenna?"

"I'm still here. Hadn't you noticed?"

"We have to talk."

"Uh-oh. Are you dumping me?"

"Certainly not. But, given your decision to be Jenna again, you will have to face some realities."

"I've been Jenna all my life, and I managed it pretty well. Except for the marriage to Wallace, I mean."

"These realities are going to be new ones."

"Enumerate them, please."

"First of all, Lance, on hearing your plans, has withdrawn from the picture."

"What picture is that?"

"The entire picture. Since you are no longer a congressional ward, as it were, you are outside of government protection."

"Government protection was a pain in the ass," she said, "and I won't be sorry to see it go."

"Well, you're still going to need protection, but you're going to have to start paying for it yourself. If you're going to Key West, you're going to need a security squad of, I'd say, eight."

"Why so many?"

"You'll need two at a time to guard you, and they all have to sleep, eat, and entertain themselves."

"How much is this going to cost?"

"You'll have to speak to Mike Freeman about that."

"How long will I need this security?"

"Until Wallace and his minions have demonstrably stopped trying to kill you. I'm not sure that's possible to predict."

"Well, life is unpredictable, isn't it?"

"Yes, it is. I'll do what I can to set this up for you. And I'll supply transportation and the house."

"Thank you, that's very kind, Stone. But at some point, of your choosing, I'd like you to send me a bill."

"I don't want to see you bleed away your fortune."

"You're forgetting something," she said.

"What am I forgetting?"

"Jamie."

"Well, you'll need to decide how to dispose of her ashes . . ."

"That's not what I mean. Our parents, both now dead, divided their estate between us, so we each got half their money. Now I will inherit Jamie's share."

"I'll have an estate attorney from Woodman & Weld do the legal work on that."

"And Jamie was a much bolder investor than I, so her share, I think, has doubled."

Stone thought about that. "So, you're saying that your net worth will now be something around or over two hundred million? The attorney will determine that."

"My point is that I can afford to pay for your work, your airplane, and for the security detail you're proposing."

"All right, at an appropriate time, I'll bill you, and so will Strategic Services."

"I'm glad we've settled that. Now, how am I going to tell the world that I am alive and Jamie is dead?"

"I think you are going to need a publicist," Stone said. "I can recommend a good one."

"What will he do?"

"She. She will know exactly how to make the world aware of your, ah, status, and she will handle all the media inquiries while you hide in Key West."

"'Hide'?"

"Jenna, if the media knows where to find you, they'll turn your life into a living hell. Your photograph will be in every publication and on every TV news show in the nation."

"How long will I have to hide?"

"The best person to tell us that will be the publicist. I think that one of the things she will want you to do is to subject yourself to a probing interview that will answer all the questions that people want answers to. Once they know the answers, you will gradually fade from the national interest."

"How . . ."

"Weeks, perhaps a few months, and you cannot walk the streets of Key West, or any other municipality, during that time because you would be recognized and harassed."

"How will I occupy myself?"

"My library will be at your disposal, and there are enough TVs in the house for you to catch up on hundreds of old movies, athletic events, and home-improvement techniques, not to mention shopping for small household appliances. Then, toward the end of your, ah, confinement, you can decide where you want to live and start shopping for real estate."

"You make it sound like I'll be a nun."

"Sort of."

"And what am I going to do for sex?"

Busted, Stone thought.

"Are my security guards going to provide that service?"

"Not contractually," he replied. "I suppose you'll have to play that by ear. Tell me, is there an old beau or two who might visit now and then?"

"Well, let's see," she said. "Yes! There's you!"

"I'm only one man," Stone said, "and I have a life, a dog, several houses, and a law practice to attend to. Mind you, I'm not opting out. I'll come to see you when I can, but it won't be twice a day, like now. Not even twice a month."

"I'm going to have to think about this," she said.

"Please do that."

34

Charlayne Cole, a woman of indeterminate age, known to all as Charlie, sank into Stone's office sofa and dug out a legal pad from her voluminous purse.

"Okay, what am I here for?" she demanded. Charlie always sounded as if she had no time to talk.

"It's fairly straightforward, Charlie," Stone replied. "I'd like you to bring a dead person back to life."

"I can do that," Charlie said. "Do I get to pick the dead person?"

"Alas, no. She has already been chosen."

"A girl, eh? They're easier to resurrect than guys."

"If you say so. Her name is Jenna Jacoby."

"The dead model whose ex, the senator, offed her? No problem."

"I should point out, though, that the woman murdered in the car explosion was her sister, Jamie."

"So, the dead one is still alive? Piece of cake."

"You may recall that the AP wire moved the original story. It made every paper and TV show in the country, and a lot abroad."

"Right. We'll want to move it exactly the same way, so the same people who think she's dead won't anymore."

"There's a wrinkle, though."

"There's always a wrinkle," Charlie said. "Wrinkles are my specialty. What's hers?"

"Well, apparently, a large portion of those who heard the story, or read it, came away with the impression that her ex had offed her, as you so felicitously put it."

"Right, so we sort of have to apologize to the guy, so he won't sue my client."

"Sort of. He is, by no means, guilt-free, but since Jenna is alive, neither did he actually cause her death."

"But he did cause her sister's death?"

"He did, but we are not yet ready to establish that as a fact in a libel suit in a court of law."

"I'll concentrate on who he **didn't** off, then. And we'll leave poor Jamie for next time."

"You are so perspicacious, Charlie," Stone said.

"I'll take that as a compliment, even though I have no idea what it means."

"It's a compliment."

"What other points do I need to make?"

"In the first round, let's concentrate on the non-dead part of the story, with a mention that the lady is in seclusion and will have no further comment until an unspecified later date."

"Smart! Keep 'em hanging."

"Then, when that later time comes, she will answer every pending question, so that we can say there will be nothing further to be said on the subject."

"Perfect! I'll get her on **60 Minutes** and flog the promos half to death."

"You can get her on **60 Minutes**?"

"Are you kidding? When I get through with them, they'll be begging for a glimpse of her ankle."

"How will you do that?"

"I'll force them to put her on, maybe for the whole show."

"I don't think she'll have that much to say. I'll settle for a whole segment."

"You don't start negotiations with a settlement on your lips. Trust me to get it done. How's the kid looking?"

"Let's find out," Stone said, pressing Joan's button. "Will you send in Jenna?" he asked.

"Here she comes!"

The door behind Stone's desk was flung open, and Jenna swept into the room, in much the same way that the late Loretta Young had on her old TV show.

"Jenna, this is Charlie Cole, your new publicist."

"How do you do?"

"Get your ass over here, kiddo. Let's get a good look at you."

Jenna approached the sofa, and Charlie tilted the lampshade to bathe her in light. "She'll do," Charlie said. "Congratulations, sweetie, we're going to reintroduce you to the world!"

"She's already been photographed for a future **Vogue** by Harry Benson, for a mother/daughter special issue."

"As the daughter, I hope."

"No, as the mother, but a beautiful one, though."

"I wish I'd gotten my hands on Harry before it was shot. I'll make him give me a gander at the negative, so we can see what's what."

"I don't think they have negatives anymore, Charlie," Stone said.

"You know what I mean. I'll see that she looks great."

"I know you will."

Charlie walked around Jenna. "So, Wally didn't off you, huh?"

"Nope."

"Sorry about your sister."

"Thank you."

"Now, Charlie, when can you get started?"

"How about three seconds from now? Three seconds work for you?"

"I can do three seconds."

"Three, two, one, you got some bedrooms upstairs, right? I need to get Jenna in one, sit her down, and explain things to her."

"She's leaving town for an undisclosed location tomorrow," Stone said. "She's all yours until then."

"Key West, I assume? Good choice, Stone. It's where I'd send her." She grabbed Jenna by the wrist and marched her through the door, slamming it behind her.

Joan came into Stone's office. "Was that live or recorded?" she asked.

"Live from my office," Stone replied.

"I've never heard anything like it!"

"Stick around. Charlie is just getting started."

35

Stone's aircraft touched down at Key West, then taxied to his hangar, where, by pre-arrangement, everybody, including Bob, deplaned into two waiting cars. Fifteen minutes later they spilled into the courtyard of Stone's house and were assigned to their rooms, while Bob, nose to the ground, searched the property for small, furry creatures and iguanas, then settled for one from a basket of stuffed animals.

Stone showed Jenna her half of the dressing room and the rest of the master suite, which was in its own cottage.

"So this is my prison," she said.

"For the duration," Stone replied. "You may not break cover, unless disguised and escorted."

"'The duration,'" she said aloud to herself. "That was how long World War II took, wasn't it?"

"Yes. But this duration will be much, much shorter than that one."

"So you say," she said.

"Do you feel fully briefed by Charlie Cole?"

"I feel overstuffed—sated, you might say."

"She knows whereof she speaks," Stone said.

"Oh, I know that, but I don't have to like it, do I?"

"It will be a lot more fun if you can learn to like it."

"How long can you stay?" she asked.

"One, perhaps two nights The ruse will only work if I'm seen to be at my regular station, while you are not."

Jenna started to remove clothing.

"We have no curtains in here," Stone said. "You have to remember to close the blinds." He demonstrated, then started working on his own buttons.

Soon he was introducing her to the bed, which helpfully was exactly like the beds in his other houses.

After they had consumed each other, they lay panting on their backs.

"I forgot to tell you, Stone. This is a very lovely place, perhaps the nicest prison I have ever occupied."

"I'm glad you find it so." His phone rang, and he picked it up. He covered the phone with a hand. "It's Dino. I'll have to take this."

She rolled out of bed and wandered into the large bathroom to explore the plumbing.

"Hey," Stone said into the phone.

"You landed safely? No small-arms fire?"

"Yes, no. No Hellfire missiles, either."

"When are you back?"

"Tomorrow, the next day."

"Are you going to the Yacht Club for dinner tonight?"

"Nope. Jenna must remain unknown and unsighted here. We'll cook or order in."

"When does Charlie's bombshell hit the airwaves?"

"In three days. I want to be back in the city by then to personally deny all the rumors. That's Charlie's idea. She thinks it's better than just issuing a statement."

"Charlie knows."

"She does."

———

They grilled steaks that night. The next night Anna cooked a large Polish stew of some sort for Stone's last night in town.

Jenna was even more demanding on that last night. The following morning, Stone hobbled to the car and was delivered inside his hangar. A half hour later, he and Bob were on their way back to New York.

———

On what Charlie had designated the "pub date," Stone's phone started ringing very early, but he threw a blanket over it while he got himself together and had breakfast.

Joan was waiting for him downstairs. She handed him a typed sheet of paper. "These are the ones who can't be denied. You want to start with Henry, at Page Six?"

"Nah, the **Times**, then the **Wall Street Journal**, then Page Six."

He got through the first two quickly, then gritted his teeth for Henry.

"She's in Key West, right?" Henry asked.

"Henry, three days ago I delivered her into the hands of persons unknown to me, and they delivered her to God knows where. I mentioned Key West, but she said it was too hot for her there. If I were guessing, I'd start a lot farther north."

"You're just trying to confuse me."

"Why not? **I'm** confused. I don't expect to see her again until her ex-husband has expired or gone gaga, which a lot of people think he is doing as we speak."

"Can I quote you on that?"

"Henry, you're going to quote me no matter what I say. And you'll probably make up most of it. Gotta run, your competitors are on the phone."

"Tell them to go fuck themselves."

"Can I quote you on that?" Stone hung up and took the next call. By noon they were down to a trickle, and Joan put everybody on hold while he had a corned beef sandwich. At mid-afternoon he told Joan to tell callers he was no longer available, then went to take a nap, rubbing his neck where the phone had been cradled. He had to get one of those headsets, he thought.

———

"How was your day?" Dino asked Stone over the phone.

"Don't ask. I ran out of smart-ass answers pretty quick. It was hard slogging, let me tell you. There isn't enough money to get me to do what Charlie Cole does."

"Do you think anybody knows where Jenna is?"

"Henry from Page Six rattled me when he guessed Key West right at the start. I told him she was too hot-natured for the Keys. I've no idea if it worked."

36

Stone's house phone rang again. "Hmmf?"

"You're napping already?" Charlie Cole demanded. Charlie never just asked.

"They wore me out, Charlie. I took about three thousand calls this morning."

"You may have taken thirty. Leave the hyperbole to me."

"Well, it **seemed** like three thousand. Anyway, it'll spread across the country."

"I'm doing a running check on that. We're even with the first piece, and I think we'll do better."

"Whatever happen to hearsay?"

"Oh, don't worry. They'll be gathered at every watercooler in the USA, guzzling. Then everybody will have to pee at the same time, which may put a strain on the national plumbing grid."

"Any word of any kind from Wallace Slade?"

"Not a peep, which means he's scared shitless. He doesn't know what she knows about Jamie's death in the car, but he knows she knows. Half the calls he's getting are going to be asking about Jamie. Don't worry, we'll get Jenna off the hook and Wallace onto it—at the same time."

"A twofer?"

"At the very least. Maybe a threefer. There's always Harley Quince."

"Whatever you say, Charlie."

"I like the sound of that." She hung up.

Dino called. "Is it working?"

Stone told him about Charlie's call.

"It sounds great, but you know she's probably full of shit, don't you?"

"Don't say things like that—not when she's working for me, anyway."

"Okay, she's full of your shit."

"In that case, she's telling God's truth to the nation."

"Do you think the nation can handle God's truth?"

"That, like everything else in my life, remains to be seen."

"Well, you're asking them to think the worst of somebody, and the nation is good at that."

"We do have that on my side. We've kept me off the airwaves, so the nation won't confuse me with Wallace Slade."

"Good idea. I wouldn't like you as a Republican senator from Texas."

"I know. I'd have to shoot myself. Gotta run."

"Yeah, you get back to your nap." Dino hung up.

As Stone was drifting off, his cell rang. "Yeah?"

"Scramble."

"Already done."

"Would you like a report from abroad?"

"Yes, please!"

"The European and British papers have gone nuts with the story. Even Rupert Murdoch's papers are on board with it. Wallace is slipping with the rags he can usually count on. His credibility ratings are in the toilet."

"I knew God put me on this earth for something," Stone replied. "I just didn't realize how much fun it would be."

"I don't suppose you tuned in to Fox News this morning?"

"Whenever I try to do that, my TV resists and changes to the repair-your-own-motorcycle channel."

"Lucky you. Where do I get a TV like that?"

"In heaven, and you don't want to go there, yet."

"Hope your luck holds."

"Me, too."

Lance hung up.

———

Stone was awake now, and he had no more calls to make, except one. He called Jenna.

"Is it really you?"

"It is. I spent the first half of the day fencing with the media."

"How'd you do?"

"Bloodied, but unbowed."

"How'd Wallace do?"

"Worse than I, from all available reports."

"I've seen the **Times** and **USA Today**, plus the **Key West Citizen**."

"Did they claim you as a native Key Wester?"

"Not yet."

"Good. That means they don't know you're in town, which is what we want. If they start referring to you as a conch, then we'll have to move you to another city."

"I'm not ready to go. I'm liking it here."

"No nude sunbathing by the pool, unless that's the way you want your security to see you. The caretaker, George, could turn up at an inopportune moment, too."

"I could do worse."

"Are you really keeping your head down?"

"Just the way I promised."

"Then I'll expect it to still be attached to your shoulders next time I see you."

"Which will be when?"

"To be determined. I'll do my best. Bye."

"Bye."

The TV was on, but the sound off. Suddenly, the flabby face of Senator Wallace Slade appeared on-screen. Stone fumbled for the remote control.

". . . want to say, here and now, that I know nothing of the death of Jamie Jacoby, who was one of the people I loved best on the earth."

"Don't you watch TV and read the papers?" A reporter shouted from off camera.

"I stand by what my statement was!" Slade shouted back. "Don't you try to twist my words, you son of a bitch."

"I'm just a bitch," she shouted back, "and I'm trying to untwist your words into something resembling the English language."

"We speak American in Texas! I guess that's why you're so confused."

"Where were you when Jamie's car exploded?" a male reporter yelled.

"I was driving a herd up from Texas to the railhead in Missouri!"

"I'm not talking about your campaign commercial!"

"Then you better learn to say what you mean!" Slade yelled, then walked off camera.

"Has that poor horse died yet?" the female reporter screamed after him.

The female reporter's image replaced that of Slade's. "If he's ever tried in court for murder, he'd better not defend himself!" she shouted.

The camera went back to the studio, where the two news anchors dissolved in laughter.

S tone and Dino had dinner at Georgette's
and split a goose.

As the main course arrived, so did another place setting. By the time it was in place,
Lance was sitting in front of it. "Good evening,"
he said.

"What on earth are you doing here, Lance?"

"Georgette's goose is too much for two people.
I thought I'd help out."

"And I was thinking about goose sandwiches
for lunch tomorrow," Stone said.

"You won't have time for lunch tomorrow,"
Lance said. "The funeral."

"Why not?" Stone asked. "I mean, whose funeral? Answer that one first."

"Why, Jamie's funeral or, as people prefer to

call it these days, 'memorial service,' where her friends can celebrate her life after she's dead. There won't be a casket, just a plain silver urn from Cartier."

"I didn't know Cartier was in the urn business," Dino said.

"You lead a sheltered life, Dino," Lance said, sympathetically.

"Wait a minute," Stone said. "Let's rewind for a minute. How is this funeral happening?"

"You should ask yourself that question, Stone. After all, you made it happen."

"Charlie Cole is behind all this, isn't she?"

"No, Charlie is right out in front, leading like a drum majorette. That leaves only Jenna to get behind and push, and you, yourself, to get out of the way."

"And when was I supposed to hear about this?"

"Why, the invitation has been engraved and is on your desk as we speak."

"You put it there, didn't you?"

"Stone, my firm does not operate a delivery service for messages from the beyond."

"And where, may I ask, is Jenna?"

"At another restaurant just as good as this one. Celebrating, I should imagine. Her Strategic Services detail are the hosts, so she's well protected." Lance chewed a bit. "My, this goose is plump and tender and perfectly cooked."

Stone tried it and could not disagree.

"I'll bet we're eating better than Jenna is," Dino said.

———

Stone got home and found the envelope on his desk. Scrawled across it was a message: **Don't bother to RSVP, just show up.**

He went upstairs to find Jenna curled up in his bed, quite naked.

"Well, hello there, as we say in Texas."

"You're not a Texan, are you?"

"Only as a punishment from a husband who hated me. I hail from Connecticut, a tiny village called Roxbury."

"Tell me how all this happened."

"Let's wait a bit. I think you'll appreciate it more after we've reconnected."

"Ever the optimist," Stone said.

But Jenna was right. Twice. And Stone was asleep before he could speak again.

———

They were eating breakfast.

"Charlie called and opined that we were just wasting time, with me sequestered in Key West, when we could be making noise in New York, where it counts."

"How did she transport you and your menage?"

"We grabbed hold of a passing Strategic Services jet, and wham-bam-thank-you-ma'am, we were at Teterboro. Charlie brought me to film **60 Minutes** and then the boys threw me a little wrap party at Patroon—nobody wanted you there to breathe gloom and doom around, like a joy extinguisher. Then Charlie dropped me here. I still have my remote control for the garage and my key to the house. And you, you had a busy night!"

"I'll never know how you managed that, until you've shown me again a couple of times."

"Count on it, but right now, I'm saving myself for the funeral and the cameras."

———

They made a well-planned entrance, as Fred delivered them to the front doors of the Little Church of the Twinkling Star, a name Stone found cloying, but he had to admit it suited the occasion. It was packed with a lot of people he didn't know and a few he did. Some of both made short speeches, then Jenna thanked them all and spoke about Jamie's sweetness and generosity. She held her emotions to a single, effectively managed teardrop, which every camera, still and live action, caught. The special lighting helped. Charlie Cole had apparently sprung for—or at least Stone had—the best lighting director on Broadway.

———

After the service, Stone arrived home with Jenna to find that he was hosting a lush luncheon for thirty or forty of the most favored funeral guests in his living room, dining room, and study. And the caterers were using the good china and crystal, too.

———

Afterward, the house was improbably still and silent.

"Where is your security detail?" Stone asked.

"At home with their families or out on the town, whichever they prefer. Charlie says I'm no longer a target, because if Wallace tried again everybody in the country would know who did it."

"I hate to admit it, but Charlie is one hell of a security consultant, in addition to whatever else she does."

"Freedom through publicity!" Jenna laughed, and they went up to bed.

38

Stone was awakened by Jenna's cell phone. "Yes? Wow! Will anybody see it? Oh, good! Thanks, Charlie!" She hung up. "That was Charlie," she said.

"Who else?" Stone muttered, trying to go back to sleep.

"They're moving us to tonight," she said.

"Who's moving us up, and what is it? Have you bought furniture?"

"**Sixty Minutes**. It was supposed to run next Sunday, but they've moved it to tonight, right after the football game. Tom Brady is playing, so they'll have a huge audience, and they'll be promoting it at every time-out!"

"Do we have to do anything?"

"Just watch."

"Good. Wake me when it starts." He pulled a pillow over his ears.

Jenna elbowed him in the ribs.

"Ooof!"

"I'm hungry."

Stone picked up the phone and called downstairs. He had just gotten back to sleep when the dumbwaiter went off. Jenna served them and he managed to eat it. They watched CBS's **Sunday Morning**, and there were promos for Jenna's interview throughout.

"Well," Stone said. "Nobody's going to get through the day without hearing about your interview."

"Charlie says that's the way God intended it."

"Charlie would know that."

———

They watched. Jenna looked just great on television, and she seemed eager to tell her story, and not in the least nervous.

As they got nearer to the conclusion, Lesley Stahl leaned in and said, "Jenna, do you think it's someone you know who is trying to harm you?"

"Let me put it this way, Lesley," Jenna said. "I've racked my memory and made a list of everyone I know who would want me dead, and there's only one name on the list, and he's at the very top."

The screen faded and went to commercial.

"That was a brilliant last line," Stone said.

"I worked on it all afternoon," she said.

"Well, that worked."

Stone's phone rang. "Hello?"

"It's Charlie," she said.

"Charlie," Stone said, "take some deep breaths and slow down. You'll have a coronary!"

"Already been there," Charlie said. "I've got six other network shows who want Jenna. Oprah wants Jenna!"

"Who? I didn't quite get the name."

"OPRAH WANTS JENNA. So does Dr. Phil and Judge Judy!"

"What does Judge Judy want to try her for?"

"She has a talk show, dummy!"

"Forgive me, I'm one of the slow few who does not watch afternoon TV. Are you going to get her on a soap?"

"Right now, she could have her own soap, if she wanted it."

"Do you want to speak to Jenna?"

"I don't have time! Phil Donahue is on the other line, and he wants to make a comeback! Tell Jenna everything I said, so I won't have to repeat myself!" She hung up.

"Did you get all that?" Stone asked Jenna.

"I can have my own soap? Wow!"

"Oh, stop it. I think that what Charlie said, in

a nutshell, is that your interview touched every base, after you knocked it out of the park."

"What do you think Wallace will do?"

"My bet is, after this, Wallace Slade will turn himself in and plead guilty," Stone said.

"Oh, you! I just want to know if this will get him off my back?"

"I think it might get him out of the country," Stone said. "Does he have his own jet and a condo in the Bahamas?"

"No, but he knows people who do."

"Then he's probably on his way."

Dino called. "That was fabulous!" he said. "I hope the DA was watching."

"If he wasn't, the **New York Times** will explain it to him tomorrow morning."

"I hope Harley Quince saw it," Dino said.

That stopped Stone in his tracks. "I'll give you three to one he was watching the football game, and in that case, how could he possibly miss **60 Minutes**?"

"Sometimes I like the way your mind works," Dino said.

Jenna was waving both hands at Stone.

"What?"

"Was he talking about Harley Quince?"

"Yes, we think he must have seen the interview."

"He could still be a threat."

"How?"

"Wallace used to say that Harley was like a

firehose. Once he had turned him on, it was im-
possible to shut him off."

"I heard that," Dino said. "Well, Stone, you're
not still knee-deep in shit, but it's still up to your
ankles, and it doesn't smell any better."

39

Harley Quince had, indeed, watched the football game and seen all the promos for **60 Minutes**. But he was still surprised when Jenna popped onto the screen, and he was held rapt as she was interviewed. At the end, when Jenna said she had a list of one who hated her, he figured she was talking not about the senator, but him. And he did not enjoy being discussed in such terms on national television.

He was inclined to get out his nine millimeter and fire a few rounds into her image on the TV, but when he thought about how much he had paid for the instrument, he thought better of it.

Still, she wasn't going to get away with dragging

his name through the mud, even if he deserved it. He packed some things, then got onto Amtrak for Pennsylvania Station.

———

By the time Harley reached New York, Jenna—free as a bird—was sacking Bergdorf's and filling the rear seat and trunk of Stone's Bentley with boxes and shopping bags. She called Stone on the way home.

"Yep?"

"I've just bought a new dress," she said. "Can we have dinner somewhere tonight where I can wear it?"

"Sure. How about the Carlyle's restaurant?"

"Perfect!"

———

They were set down at the Seventy-Sixth Street entrance to the hotel, heeding Stone's native caution.

"Oh, I wanted to make a splash," Jenna said. He stopped her at the entrance to the restaurant, which was packed. "There," he said, "make a splash." Not only did she do that, Stone reflected, but she got a standing O from the restaurant's patrons.

Settled in a chair where the sight lines from every table to Jenna were unimpeded, she reigned for the whole evening. The famous and the semi-famous stopped by the table, shook her and ignored Stone, which was okay with him.

———

It was late when they piled into the Bentley, and Stone was immediately on alert. "Motorcycle on your left, Fred."

"I got him, sir. I'll squash him like a bug if he makes a wrong move," Fred said, adjusting his rearview mirror.

Jenna reached out for the window switch. "I need some air," she said.

"No!" Stone said, catching her wrist. "That window is all that's between you and a bullet. I'll give you more air-conditioning." He played with the knobs, and she stopped fanning herself.

"I don't know what you're so nervous about," Jenna said. "I'm a free woman and bulletproof!"

"How many drinks have you had?" Stone asked.

"Who's counting?" she asked, reaching for the switch again. This time she was too quick for him, and the window slid a third of the way down before he could stop it.

Fred made the car do a little dance, and a rear fender caught the motorcycle and crowded it into a passing delivery truck, but not before there were two **pfft**s, and two splash marks appeared on the inside of Stone's window. He got the offending window up quickly.

"What are you doing?" Jenna demanded hotly.

Stone took her by the hair and turned her head toward his window. "Do you know what those two marks are?"

"Who cares?"

"I care. My head was right in line with them a moment ago."

"I don't understand," she said.

"The marks were made by bullets, and those **pfft** sounds you heard were from a silenced pistol."

"Oh, don't be silly!"

"I'm sending you back to Key West tomorrow," he said.

"No, no, it's too hot there! Why don't you want me to be cool?"

"I want you to sober up and think about what's going on around you," Stone said.

"Sober is no fun."

"Neither is being shot in the head. If you doubt that, just put your window down again."

"I think we're all right now, sir," Fred said. "He's still tangled up with the delivery truck. There! He's reversed course and gone the other way."

"You see?" Jenna bubbled. "There's no danger."

"He might just try for another shot," Stone said, "and you'll get a second chance to have your brains scattered all over my beautiful leather seats."

"Oh, you're more concerned with your leather seats than with my brains!"

Stone took her by the shoulders, twisted her body, and sat her down on the nice wool carpet that covered the floor. "Stay there," he commanded, "or I'll put my foot on your neck to keep you in place!"

They pulled into Stone's garage, and the door closed behind them. Jenna was out of the car like a rocket. "I will not be treated this way!" she yelled, stamping her foot for effect.

"Then sleep somewhere else besides in my bed tonight, and tomorrow morning, when you've sobered up, start packing!"

"Packing? For where?"

"Anyplace you like, except where I am," Stone said, and left her standing in the hallway outside the master suite.

40

Stone woke the following morning with the bed beside him empty. He ordered breakfast, watched **Morning Joe,** read the **Times,** and did the crossword. Jenna had not reappeared.

Dino called.

"Good morning."

"Is it? I heard Jenna was a handful at the Carlyle last night."

"You might say that. I lost count of how many drinks she had, but she was the Toast of New York for about four hours. I managed to prevent her from dancing on the table, but that was the best I could do."

"I heard there were shots fired later."

"Man on a motorcycle. Jenna kept trying to open the window to make it easier for him."

"How is she feeling this morning?"

"She hasn't surfaced yet. I suspect she's too embarrassed about her behavior last night, or maybe just too hung over."

Joan buzzed him. "Hang on, Dino. Yes, Joan?"

"Is Jenna leaving today?"

"I haven't seen her this morning. Why do you ask?"

"Because there's a pile of luggage and shopping bags by the garage door. Fred hasn't seen her, either."

"She'll turn up. Dino, you there?"

"I'm hanging. Do you want to file a missing person report?"

"Do people pack seven pieces of luggage when they're about to go missing?"

"Viv packs that much to go away for the weekend."

"No, Jenna must have forgotten to empty a couple of shops on Madison Avenue yesterday. She'll turn up."

"Whatever you say, pal."

Stone's other line rang again.

"It's Fred, sir."

"Good morning, Fred, what's up?"

"Miss Jenna drove up in a brand-new Mercedes estate wagon, the AMG one, with the window sticker still on it, and had me put all her luggage into it. Then she kissed me goodbye and drove away."

"Drove away where?"

"She didn't say. She didn't say anything at all but 'goodbye.'"

"Well," Stone said, "it sounds as if she no longer wishes to seek shelter here."

"It looks that way to me, sir."

"Since we don't know where she's going, we can't do anything about it, can we?"

"I suppose not, sir. Sorry to have disturbed you."

"You did the right thing, Fred. Now I'm going to do the right thing."

"What's that, sir?"

"Nothing." Stone hung up.

Joan buzzed again. "Fred told me."

"Yes, it sounds as though she was shopping Eleventh Avenue this morning, instead of Madison." Eleventh Avenue was where the car dealerships lived.

Stone called Dino.

"Bacchetti."

"Well, now she's officially missing," Stone said. "Apparently, she bought a new Mercedes-AMG station wagon this morning, filled it to the brim with luggage, and drove off into the sunrise."

"Now do you want me to file a missing person report?"

"No, she's a grown woman, and a rich one at that. She can go anywhere she pleases."

"If she doesn't mind being dead," Dino added.

"Well, there is that, isn't there."

———

Harley Quince arrived as the luggage was being loaded by Fred, but he didn't see Jenna. Then Fred caught sight of him and gave him a hard stare, so he accelerated out of there. He drove around the corner, executed a U-turn against traffic, turned back into the block, and stopped. The Mercedes wagon was gone. That luggage hadn't looked as though it had belonged to Barrington, so it must have been Jenna's, Quince reasoned. He tore up the street to the next corner and looked both ways: the Mercedes was a block up Park Avenue, with its left blinker on. Quince accelerated after it, threading his way through the dense traffic.

———

Fred had witnessed Quince's action from the garage door, and there was no time to get the Bentley out, so he grabbed Stone's little-used Norton motorcycle, got it started, and roared out of the garage, turning toward Park Avenue. Fred stopped, lowered the kickstand, stood on the bike seat, and surveyed the traffic; he saw the wagon turn left on Fifty-Seventh Street, so he dropped back onto the seat, retracted the kickstand, and headed uptown, not bothering with traffic lights or outraged cabdrivers who didn't like to be passed on their left, next to the center garden area.

Fred muscled the bike onto West Fifty-Seventh Street and saw the black motorcycle and its black-clad rider a block ahead and two blocks behind the Mercedes. Jenna apparently had a heavy foot, and she was driving a very powerful car, so the black motorcycle was having a hard time gaining on her. Fred could keep up with the other bike, though.

Then there was an accident at the corner of Madison Avenue, and the black cycle was momentarily trapped. Fred turned behind a FedEx truck and onto the sidewalk, scattering pedestrians, and made it all the way to Fifth Avenue, where he turned into Jenna's lane. She stopped for a traffic light. "Thank God," Fred said aloud to himself and poured it on until he screeched to a halt outside her window. He rapped on the window and she turned and looked at the man in the helmet, horrified. She was digging in her purse for something, and Fred was very much afraid it was a pistol.

He unbuckled the chin strap and pulled off the helmet. "Ms. Jenna!" he shouted.

She froze for a moment, then said or, rather, mouthed, **Fred?** Her window slid down.

"There's a black motorcycle behind you, miss. The one from last night, I'm afraid."

"What should I do?" she asked.

"You proceed as planned, and I'll deal with him."

The light changed and she roared away. Fred looked over his shoulder and saw the black motorbike coming his way.

41

Fred watched the Mercedes-AMG rocket away from him, turning right on Sixth Avenue. He negotiated his way around a bus and followed as best as he could. He had no idea what had become of the black motorcycle.

Then Fred looked up and saw Central Park South, which bordered the park, rushing at him, and Jenna was showing no signs of turning. Did she know that the road through Central Park was closed to all traffic more boisterous than a horse-drawn carriage? Apparently not, because she went straight ahead into the park, narrowly avoiding a carriage, and began to scatter joggers, who were pointing and screaming at the disappearing station wagon. She was going to kill somebody.

Fred did his best to avoid the runners, then

watched as Jenna turned left on East Sixty-Sixth Street, which still supported two-way auto traffic across the park. She blew straight through the traffic light at Central Park West, and Fred followed in her wake. She turned right at the next corner, then left on West Seventy-Second Street.

Did she have a plan, Fred asked himself, or was she just running? As he turned left on Seventy-Second, he looked over his shoulder and saw the black motorcycle still doggedly in pursuit a block back. A chorus of car horns wafted uptown, and Fred heard them.

Jenna had accelerated and she was crossing major streets like Broadway, then again running a light at Riverside Drive. The next choice was the street turning left and downtown, or a right onto the Henry Hudson Parkway, and for the first time, Jenna hesitated and appeared to be making a decision. To Fred's relief, she turned right onto the parkway and stood on it, parting traffic. Fred took the precaution of actually looking for traffic on his left before following.

If Jenna had had a siren, she would be using it now, and astonishingly, no police vehicle had taken notice of her. She was staying in the left lane with her emergency flashers on and leaning on the horn. Terrified drivers tried desperately to get out of her way.

Fred's immediate attention was drawn to his windshield, where a bullet hole had appeared.

He looked to his left and saw the black cycle and its driver with a semiautomatic pistol in his left hand. Fred did what he thought would not be expected of him and leaned left. The black-clad driver stomped on his brakes and avoided a collision, but in his rearview mirror, Fred could see that he no longer held the pistol. In the commotion, he seemed to have dropped it.

Fred braked and came up to the other cycle's right. He turned quickly left, and the black-clad driver was scraping along the steel medial railing. Sparks were flying, and he dropped back farther.

Fred took advantage of the moment and accelerated, looking for Jenna's Mercedes. She was, perhaps, a quarter-mile ahead, and he asked of the Norton all that it could give.

Slowly he gained ground, and then, after they had passed under the George Washington Bridge, which spanned the Hudson River, he managed to pull even with her on her right side. The Harlem River bridge looked ahead of them now, and his efforts to flag her down had failed. The road narrowed at the tollbooths, and he fell behind her. Tolls had been overtaken by E-ZPass, so they were uninhibited. Fred mused that the automatic cameras would have some truly remarkable photographs today. Their two vehicles were now doing ninety miles per hour.

Past the George Washington Bridge even Jenna

had to slow, if eighty could be considered slow, because of the curvy nature of the road. Then the road straightened as they merged with the Saw Mill River Parkway, and Jenna was doing a hundred. Approaching Yonkers, Fred's Norton hiccupped, and he looked at the gauge to find it on nearly empty. He jammed on the brakes and exited at Executive Parkway, where he knew there was a gas station near the exit. He ended up pushing the bike the last block. Then, while his tank was filling, he called his boss.

"Fred?"

"Yes, sir," Fred panted.

"You sound as though you've been running," Stone said.

"In a manner of speaking, sir, I have. I ran short on fuel and lost her, headed north on the Saw Mill, at a great rate of knots."

"You chased her that far?"

"Yes, sir, and at times we were doing the century."

"Good God! What about the other bike, the black one?"

"I jammed him into the guardrail south of the GW Bridge, and he seemed to drop out."

"Do you have any idea where she's headed?"

"Sir, the only place I can think of would be your house in Washington, Connecticut. She knows about it, doesn't she?"

"Yes, but I sold the place to Bill Eggers."

"You might try calling her and telling her that, sir."

"I'll do that. Did your chase interest the police at all?"

"Amazingly, no, sir. I never saw a copper, never heard a siren. I wished for one, though."

"I can imagine. Come home, Fred. Keep your speed down and take another route. Don't attract any attention."

"What do we do about Ms. Jenna?"

"She seems hell-bent on killing herself. Let's hope that doesn't happen. I can't think of anything else to do."

Fred paid for his gas and headed home on surface streets. He did not catch sight of the black motorcycle.

42

Jenna merged from the Saw Mill River Parkway onto I-684, and traffic began to thicken, slowing her. Her cell phone rang, and she automatically answered it. "Hello?"

"It's Stone," he said. "Please listen and don't hang up. I don't know if you're aware of this, but you were pursued from my house by a black motorcycle."

"Yes," she said. "Fred told me and then he stayed after me."

"He was just trying to keep you from killing yourself. I don't think the black bike was of that sympathy, though."

"What should I do?"

"You seem to be headed, more or less, to

Washington, Connecticut, but you should know that I've sold my house there to my colleague, Bill Eggers, and he's not there. There is the Mayflower Inn, though, a short distance away, and that could be a good place for you to stop."

"It's a thought."

"Would you like me to ask Joan to book you a room?"

She thought about it. "I'd prefer a suite."

"We'll ask for that. If you don't hear back from me in the next fifteen minutes, consider it booked."

"Thank you."

"Put the Mayflower into your GPS, and it will guide you there."

"All right, thank you." She hung up and performed the task.

Stone hung up, and Joan was standing by his desk. "A suite at the Mayflower for Jenna?"

"Yes, please."

"Will you be joining her?"

"I wasn't invited."

———

Jenna found the Mayflower and presented herself at the front desk.

"Ms. Jacoby? I believe you've booked a suite," the young lady said.

"Yes, please."

"Have you any luggage?"

Jenna gave her the car key. "Quite a lot of it," she said.

"The bellman will attend to it. Shall I show you upstairs?"

"Just give me directions." She found the suite and let herself in. It was handsome and comfortably furnished. Her luggage arrived shortly. She put her things in the dressing room and stretched out on the bed. Shortly, she was asleep.

———

Her pursuer pulled his bike off the pavement of the parking lot at the Mayflower, concealing the machine as well as he could. He saw Jenna go inside, and a moment later, a bellman with a cart took all her luggage inside.

He got out of his leathers and took some street clothes from his saddlebags and changed. He donned a tweed cap and walked across the parking lot and inside. He went to the front desk and asked, "Has Jenna Jacoby arrived yet? I was following her from the city, but I got lost."

"Yes, she has," the young woman said. "Is she expecting you?"

"It was meant to be a surprise," he said. "Have you a single room for the night?"

She checked.

"I'll have that," he said. He was shocked at the

price, but the senator was paying, so what the hell? He registered as Jason Bell.

"Any luggage?"

"No, I'm traveling light. Perhaps you could let me have a toothbrush and a razor." Soon he was ensconced, but the desk clerk wouldn't give him Jenna's room number.

———

Stone called the manager of the Mayflower, who he knew. "Jenna Jacoby has checked into a suite there, hasn't she?"

"Yes, Mr. Barrington."

"Has anyone asked for her at the front desk?"

"Please hold, I'll find out." He returned shortly. "Yes, a gentleman checked in a few minutes after she did. He said he'd been following her from New York and had gotten lost. Should we be concerned about him?"

"Yes, you should. Of course, he could be a harmless autograph seeker, but he could also be a threat to her life."

"How can we help?"

"Here's what I think you should do," Stone said, and he told him.

43

Stone called Mike Freeman, at Strategic Services, and explained the situation.

"How should I handle this, Mike?"

"Well, Quince is not wanted for any crime in Connecticut, and he has no arrest record there. Any action you take would be outrageously illegal, and you could be charged with a crime. Listen, you're the lawyer here. Why am I having to tell you this?"

"I just thought you might have an idea."

"Shooting him in the head is an effective action. Kidnapping less so, but no less illegal. Are you seeing my point?"

"I am, Mike."

"Are you in communication with Jenna?"

"Sometimes."

"What does that mean?"

"It means that sometimes she won't talk or listen to me. Also, the cell service is spotty up there."

"I suggest that you call her on the hotel's landline, explain the situation, and tell her my people are on the way, with arrival in about three hours. I'll wait to hear from you on that last one."

"All right, Mike, thanks for your help." Stone called the hotel and asked for Jenna.

"What?" she said sleepily.

"It's Stone. Harley Quince, or someone very like him, has followed you to Connecticut on a motorcycle and intends to do you harm. I can dispatch guards from Strategic Services and have them on station in about three hours. How would you like to proceed?"

"I have already loaded and cocked my weapon and can use it at a moment's notice."

"Jenna, have you ever shot anyone?"

"Just once, but not to kill."

"Do you think you can just point your weapon at a man and squeeze off a round?"

"I don't know, but if what you're telling me is true, it's time to find out. It would be self-defense, wouldn't it?"

"Jenna, I think I may have said this to you before, but to be sure you understand, I'll say it again. In a situation like this the worst possible thing you can do is shoot someone. Even if you don't kill him, your life will change forever and for the worse. You will be arrested, charged, and required to put up a very high bail. By the time you're free, every media outlet in three states will be waiting for you outside the jail, to photograph you in your worst state: dirty, unkempt, wrinkled, and looking as if you slept the previous night on a park bench. Those pictures will be lurking in computers worldwide, waiting for the moment you do something you wouldn't ordinarily do. You won't be able to so much as buy a new pair of shoes without being swamped with photographers. Are you getting the picture?"

"I think so."

"The best possible thing you can do for yourself right now is to unload your weapon, lock your door, and take a three-hour nap. By that time professionals will be dealing with all this."

"Oh, all right!" She slammed down the phone.

Stone called back Mike Freeman.

"Yes, Stone?"

"I read her the riot act, and she may have acquiesced. Send your men, and look out for a big black BMW motorcycle in the parking lot or woods around the inn."

"All right, then what?"

"Sit on her. I'll be there as soon as possible. Maybe I can talk her off the ledge again."

"We'll count on that," Mike said, then hung up.

Stone called the manager of the Mayflower

and brought him up to date, then he called
Bill Eggers.

"Hello."

"Bill, it's Stone. I need a favor?"

"How much?"

"Not that kind of favor. I need to borrow your
house for two or three days."

"And where should I reside during this visit?"

"Not the Greenwich house, the Washington
house."

"I don't have a house in Washington, but
you do."

"Your house in Washington, Connecticut, remember? The one I sold you?"

"Oh, yes. I've been meaning to speak to you
about the gutters."

"Bill, the time to speak about the gutters was
before closing, during the inspection period,
remember?"

"Well, if we're going to stand on ceremony . . ."

"Bill, we're going to stand on Connecticut real
estate law. Now listen to me: My client, Jenna
Jacoby—your client, too, the one with a net
worth of a couple of hundred million dollars?"

"Oh, yes. I remember her."

"Her life is in danger. An assassin is hunting
her. She's at the Mayflower Inn, in Washington,
and I need to get her out of there and into a safe
place. I need to borrow your house."

"Sure, anything for a client with that much

money. The key's under the flowerpot, but I'm not sure which one."

"Bill, when you moved in, did you change or rekey the locks?"

"No, it cost too much."

"Then my old key will work."

"I guess so."

"If anybody but me calls you about Jenna, deny all knowledge, got it?"

"Got it. Good luck."

Stone hung up. "Joan!" he shouted. "Roust Fred to bring around the Bentley!" He went upstairs to pack a few clothes.

44

Fred was looking sleepy, so Stone drove. He enjoyed the Saw Mill River Parkway, and he welcomed the opportunity. Twenty minutes out from the inn he called them and asked for Jenna.

"Hello?" She sounded more awake.

"It's Stone. I'll be there in twenty minutes. We're moving you to another address, so please get your things packed and have a bellman take them downstairs, but please tell him not to put them in the lobby or on the front porch. They might be recognized."

"Stone, are you sure this is really necessary?"

"I am. And be sure to unload your pistol and put it into a suitcase."

"All right."

Stone thought he heard her stamp her foot. "See you shortly," he said and hung up before she could argue further.

He made the turnoff for the Mayflower on time and drove to the hilltop parking lot, where a bellman awaited. "Don't park it," Stone said to him. "She's checking out. Have you brought down her luggage?"

"No, sir, we haven't had a call."

Stone went into the inn and found the manager at the front desk, who went upstairs with him. He knocked on the door of her suite, but there was no reply. He knocked again and shouted, "Jenna, it's Stone." Nothing.

Stone stepped aside and let the manager open the door. He found Jenna dressed but lying on the bed, asleep. He sat her up and patted her cheeks smartly. "Jenna, wake up!"

She opened her eyes and stared at him dully. "What?"

"Have you taken a sleeping pill?"

"Last night," she said.

"You only arrived earlier today, and you were wide awake." He gave up, and started putting things into her suitcase, tucking her sleeping pills into his pocket. When he turned around again, she was back asleep. He managed to get everything into her bags, and the manager called for a bellman.

Stone picked her up in his arms and was

grateful for her slimness. He got her into the elevator and pressed the lobby button. The elevator moved very slowly.

Fred was helping the bellman pack the car, and he opened a rear door and helped get Jenna inside. Stone tipped the bellman lavishly and got behind the wheel. As he was about to start the car, his cell phone rang. "Yes?"

"It's Mike. My people are on site."

"Tell them I'm in the green Bentley and to follow me. I'm moving her to my old house, a few blocks away." He started the car and got it turned around. As he did, a couple of men were pushing a large BMW motorcycle out of the woods and into the parking lot. Stone rolled down his window. "Take it down the hill and hide it in the woods there," he said. "That ought to slow the guy down."

He drove the short distance to his old house and used the key to open the front door, then he and Fred carried Jenna inside and installed her on the living room sofa. Stone put a blanket over her.

Stone sent Fred up with the bags he had packed himself, then found the Strategic Services detail leader. "How many men have you got?"

"Eight," the man replied.

"Spread half of them around the house; put the others upstairs in the bedrooms over the garage and tell them to get some sleep." He went back inside the house and made sure all the doors and windows were locked. "Fred," he said, "take the bedroom on the top floor and make yourself comfortable."

"I'm all right for the moment, sir."

Stone heard a car pull into the driveway, and found Bill Eggers getting out of a large Mercedes. "Bill, what are you doing here?"

"I went to the inn, but they said you had checked out, so I came here."

"You're not supposed to be here, Bill. I'm just borrowing your house."

"I thought you needed me," Eggers said.

"Come inside, and I'll give you some of your own whiskey."

He sat Eggers in the living room and then found him a double Scotch and himself some bourbon. "Fred, pour yourself whatever you like." Fred headed for the bar.

"Did I loan you the liquor, too?" Eggers asked, sipping his drink.

"Yes," Stone replied. "Take it out of this year's bonus."

"You expect to drink more of it?"

"I do."

"I'll make a note of it, then. What do we do now?"

"We keep a man named Harley Quince from murdering Jenna. She's the unconscious woman on the living room sofa."

"Couldn't you find her a bed?"

"Yes, but I couldn't carry her that far."

Eggers put down his drink, went to a cupboard, removed a double-barreled shotgun, loaded it, then sat down again and put the shotgun across the arms of the chair. "Ready on the firing line," he said.

"Please don't shoot anybody," Stone pleaded. "There are eight of Mike Freeman's people in or around the house and guesthouse, and you don't know any of them."

"Thanks for letting me know."

As Eggers was finishing his drink, Stone gently removed the shotgun from the arms of his chair, unloaded it, and returned the weapon and its ammo to the cupboard.

45

Harley Quince tromped through the woods, up and down the hill, until finally he found his motorcycle, concealed by piled-up brush. The sun was low in the sky, and he scrambled to get it back on the drive before darkness arrived. The machine started immediately, when asked. He drove over to the main road and tried to figure out which way the village was. He chose a right turn and drove to the top of a hill, where there stood a white Congregationalist church. He stopped and gave thought again to his direction.

———

With darkness looming, Stone ordered a dozen pizzas from the shop in the village, then hung up and beckoned the detail leader. "Will you send one of your guys to the pizza shop in the village? Down the hill, left immediately after the bridge. He'll see it." He handed the agent some cash, then took a newspaper from the dozing Eggers's lap and sat down in the living room to read it. His eye was immediately caught by the name, Slade, on the front page:

SENATOR WALLACE SLADE TO ACCEPT HONORARY DEGREE FROM UNIVERSITY

Senator Slade will, tomorrow, be accepting a prestigious Honorary Doctor of Divinity degree from the Hearthrug Bible College of Hearthrug, Connecticut, and will address what is anticipated to be a large audience there.

The ceremony will be followed by a chicken barbecue lunch on the front lawn of the college, weather permitting.

"Anybody know where Hearthrug, Connecticut, is?" he asked the room. An agent looked up from his magazine. "I saw the name on a road sign when we were driving up here, but I can't remember where that was."

Harley Quince was coasting down the hill toward what looked like a small business district, when he caught a whiff of his favorite thing: pizza. He hit the brakes and turned left toward the scent. A moment later he saw the sign PIZZA, which was a tipoff. He glided past the restaurant, looking for a parking spot. As he did, a man came out of the place with a stack of at least a dozen pizzas in his arms.

Now, he thought, who would need a dozen pizzas? Perhaps a crowd of security guards? And who, in this lovely village, would need security guards? He turned around and followed the man's pizza-laden car back up the hill, then right at the church. Then he pulled over and watched the car as it pulled into a driveway. He turned around and returned to the restaurant for a pizza of his very own.

————

Stone dealt the pizza boxes onto the kitchen counter and placed a stack of plates and napkins alongside, then found a jug of wine and unscrewed the top. He found a box of paper cups, too. "Dinner is served," he announced, and he didn't have to say it twice. The agents swarmed around the counter.

"Do I smell pizza?" a female voice asked.

Stone looked up from his plate as he devoured a slice of all-meat. "You do," he said through the pizza. "Go grab a plate." Apparently, the smell of pizza was enough to overwhelm a sleeping pill. Jenna did as she was told, unusual for her. The Power of Pizza.

———

Harley Quince finished a small pizza and washed it down with a bottle of beer, then took a deep breath. What he needed was some fresh air. He left some money on the table and went outside, sucking in the cool evening air. What he needed was moving air, he thought. He cranked up his bike and moved some air, heading back up the hill and driving slowly past the house of pizza. He parked in an empty driveway a few doors down the street, and walked back toward the house, keeping close to the hedge that bordered the street. He expected the sounds of eating and drinking from the house, but it was eerily quiet. He crept around the house and peered through a kitchen window. There were a lot of men inside, and at least half of them were asleep. Having ingested a pizza and a beer himself, he could understand that. A TV came on inside, and the sounds of football could be discerned. He found a woodshed behind the house, which contained a large kindling box, and he laid down on top of it and pulled a burlap bag over his feet. Soon, he was asleep, too.

46

Stone awoke with something on his mind, but he couldn't remember what. Jenna was of no help, being sound asleep still. His stomach spoke to him, then he remembered that he was in Bill Eggers's house, and no one was sending up breakfast in a dumbwaiter. He showered, shaved, and went downstairs, following the call of frying bacon.

Eggers was standing at the stove, wearing a colorful apron, scrambling eggs. "Just in time," he said, loading a plate and handing it to Stone. "What sort of day do you have ahead?"

"I never seem to know anymore," Stone replied. "There's a familiar-looking woman in my bed, but I can't place her."

"That would be the ex–Mrs. Wallace Slade, if memory serves."

"Ah, yes," Stone said.

"Did you see the piece in that newspaper about Slade getting an honorary doctorate from some podunk Bible college?"

"That's what I couldn't remember. Hearthrug Bible College!"

"Sounds right."

"Bill, do you have a road atlas in the house?"

"If you had one when you still owned the place, it will still be here."

"Then you don't."

"What do you want to know?"

"Where Hearthrug is."

"Google it on your iPhone."

"Ah!" Stone did so. "Here it is on the map. It's about twelve miles north of here."

"Why do you care?" Eggers asked.

"Because he's Harley Quince's master, and we know Quince is around somewhere."

"In Washington, Connecticut? Already?"

"He followed Jenna up from the city. He even had a room at the inn, and we found his motorcycle in the woods and hid it from him."

"Well, if he's still here, he's pissed off," Eggers said. "People don't like having their motorcycles hidden from them."

"You're certain of that, Bill?"

"Fairly certain. Would you?"

"I guess not."

"Where were we?" Eggers asked.

"Hearthrug Bible College."

"Oh, yes. Do you want to go up there and hear Senator Slade expel hot air?"

"Good God, no!"

"Then eat your breakfast and shut up."

The kitchen door opened and an agent came in. "Stone," he said, "there's a bum in your woodshed."

"I beg your pardon," Eggers said, "that would be **my** woodshed. Stone surrendered all legal rights to the woodshed in our sales agreement."

"It's his woodshed," Stone said, jerking a thumb at Eggers. "Make your complaint to him."

The agent turned to Eggers. "Mr. Eggers, there's a bum asleep in your woodshed."

"We can't call them bums anymore," Eggers said. "They're 'homeless' now."

"Well, one of them has made a home in your woodshed."

"How do you know this?" Eggers asked.

"Because it seemed like a nice day for a fire, but we were out of kindling, so I looked in the woodshed."

"Did you find any there?"

"Well, if you have any, it's under a homeless bum."

Stone looked up to see someone flash past a

kitchen window, headed toward the street. "Maybe not," he said. "Take another look."

When the man opened the door, they heard the sound of a motorcycle cranking up and roaring away.

"I think the kindling may be available to you now," Stone said to the agent.

"Do you have some idea who was in my woodshed?" Eggers asked.

"Harley Quince, I suspect. At least, he has a motorcycle. Who else would in this neighborhood?"

The agent came back with an armload of kindling. "Thanks for clearing the shed," he said.

"Did you get a shot at him?" Stone asked.

"What, do folks in these parts shoot at people who sleep in their woodsheds?"

"Let me put it this way," Stone said. "Would you have taken a shot at him, if you'd known he was Harley Quince?"

"Is **that** who he was?"

"It's my best guess."

"Well, shit. I could have saved us all a lot of trouble," the agent said, then continued on his journey to the fireplace with his kindling. "I'll nail the bastard next time," he called over his shoulder.

"Don't bother," Stone said. "He'd be more useful in handcuffs than dead."

"I'll make a note of that."

"Are you counting on Quince to lead you to Slade?" Eggers said.

"Not exactly. I know where to find Slade: at Hearthrug Bible College. I just want to stop Quince from killing Jenna."

"Wouldn't killing him take care of that?"

"Bill, are you forgetting that you're an attorney-at-law?"

"Well, I could turn my head for a minute, so as not to be a witness."

"I was referring to how much more trouble it is to kill somebody than to just detain him."

"I guess you have a point there," Eggers replied. "But not for Jenna, maybe."

"As it happens, she's armed, so she can take care of it herself."

"She's carrying a gun in my house? Does she have a license for it?"

"Maybe in Texas, where I think you have to be licensed **not** to carry a gun."

"Well, then, you'd better explain to your client that she shouldn't be found with that weapon in Connecticut."

"I'll be sure to do that," Stone said.

47

Stone looked up from his breakfast to find Jenna, holding a newspaper, wandering into the kitchen. "Good morning," he said. "Welcome back to the world. Would you like some breakfast?"

"Yes, thank you, I'm starved."

"The gentleman in the colorful apron will take your order," he replied, nodding toward Eggers.

"Eggs Benedict," she said.

"Not available," Eggers replied. "Available are eggs scrambled, over easy, or just fried. Sausage or bacon. Toast, if you know how to use a toaster."

"Scramble, sausage, toast, but I will not be subjected to the ignominy of operating a toaster."

Eggers looked at Stone. "Is she serious?"

"She's a client," Stone replied.

"Coming right up," Eggers said, and got busy.

"Did you see this paper?" she asked nobody in particular.

"Sort of."

"This nonsense of an honorary degree?"

"Yes."

"Where is this . . ." She consulted the paper. "Hearthrug?"

"About twelve miles from here."

"Then why don't we go there and blow him out of the water?"

"Are we sufficiently armed for that action?"

"It's a naval term for messing up his day."

"No cannon fire?"

"Only metaphorically."

"I'm willing to make that metaphorical trip," Stone said. "I don't have anything else to do today. Bill, you up for a metaphorical trip?"

Eggers handed Jenna her breakfast. "I'll check my schedule," he said. He looked at his iPhone. "Okay, I'm clear. Are we dressing, or is my apron enough?"

"Are you wearing trousers under it?" Jenna asked.

"I think so."

"Everybody dresses for Bible college," she said. "Sunday best." She sat down next to Stone and started eating.

"You can't go armed to a Bible college," Stone said. "Not in Connecticut, anyway."

"I'll pretend I'm in Texas," she said.

"Nobody will believe that."

"You'll have to surrender your weapons to the property holder," Stone said, jerking a thumb at Eggers.

"That seems extreme."

"Your legal representation requires it of you."

"What about Harley Quince?"

"He slept in our host's woodshed last night, but fled this morning, so the coast is clear. That's a naval term, meaning the coast is clear and that assignations are okay."

"I'm not looking for an assignation with Harley Quince," she said.

"I'm relieved to hear it," Stone replied. "We can just make the prestigious presentation if you can be ready to travel in an hour. We may not be able to bring carry guns, but we can hurt him in other ways."

"I'll hurry," she said.

———

They took Jenna's Mercedes-AMG, and Stone drove. "Nice ride," he said.

"It better be," she replied. "Do you know what it cost?"

"Approximately. Did you have it insured?"

"Oops."

"Do you have a household insurance policy, anywhere?"

"Yes."

"Then call your agent Monday morning and tell him about the car. Right now, while I'm driving, it's covered under my policy."

"How do you know that?"

"Because I'm on the board of the insurance company." Stone slammed on the brakes. His windshield was filled with a buck deer, who didn't even look surprised. Finally, the animal moseyed off the road.

"Lots of that in Connecticut," Stone said, resuming progress.

Soon, they could breathe again.

"Do you think Harley Quince is attending the festivities?" Eggers asked.

"He doesn't seem like the type," Stone replied.

"Wallace doesn't seem like the type, either," Jenna pointed out. "He hasn't been in a church since our wedding."

The GPS found the school, and they drove through stone and wrought-iron gates, where people who looked like Bible students directed them to parking. Stone notice that the area they had been directed to looked like a German car dealership's front lot. Stone parked, and they all got out.

"Do I have to frisk you?" Stone asked Jenna.

"As much fun as that sounds, no."

"It's bad taste to shoot somebody on Bible college property."

"I hope somebody explained that to Harley Quince," Eggers said.

They were approached by a freshly scrubbed Bible student with a crew cut. "Welcome, brothers and sister," he said to them. "Straight ahead to premium seating."

"Have we come to the Super Bowl by mistake?" Eggers asked.

They walked through an opening in a high hedge and found themselves on a lawn before a white-columned building that contained, Stone estimated, maybe four hundred folding chairs, about a hundred of which were occupied by women in filmy cotton dresses and men in seersucker suits, most of them fanning themselves with fans imprinted with funeral-home advertising.

"How long before we start?" Stone asked.

"Three minutes ago," Eggers said. "Have a seat and a fan."

A man in a blue suit stepped before the podium, which was set up on the front porch of the building ahead. "We'll give the latecomers a few more minutes to find seats," he said.

"I don't see any latecomers," Stone said, fanning himself.

"I think we're the last of the latecomers," Eggers said. As he did, a distant rumble of thunder could be heard. He whipped out his iPhone. "Let's see what Weatherbug has to say about that. Uh-oh."

"What do you mean, 'uh-oh'?" Stone got out his own phone and had a look. "Uh-oh."

"One hell of a front coming through here," Eggers said.

"I just got a text alert," Stone said. "It says thunderstorms less than ten miles away."

"Good afternoon, ladies and gentlemen, students. Welcome to the Hearthrug Bible College. I am Reverend Don Beverly Calhoun the Third, and I have the honor to be the chairman of the board of this institution." He stopped for applause and got very little for his trouble. "It is my great pleasure to be able to introduce our honored guest today, Senator Wallace Slade, who has for many years been a bulwark of conservative family values in our country."

"Ha!" Jenna emitted. People turned and looked for the source of the noise, but she smiled sweetly.

"Jenna," Stone whispered. "If you're not careful, these genteel people are going to be tearing us from limb to limb."

A clap of thunder sounded very near. Stone excused himself, went back to the car, and returned with the two golf umbrellas they had brought. He made it back as the first heavy raindrops were falling and Wallace Slade began to speak.

48

O nce Stone reached their seats he opened the two umbrellas.

"Excuse me," a man behind them said. "We can't see through your umbrellas."

Eggers turned and looked at him. "Don't worry," he said, "it won't matter in just a moment."

"I'm sorry, what do you mean?" the man said. "Of course it matters!"

A small woman ran up to Senator Slade and held a rather small umbrella over his head.

"Did you bring this weather with you?" Slade demanded of her.

"No," Stone said loudly. "We brought it with us."

Then it was as if someone had tipped over a large bucket in the sky and poured water over them all.

The people behind Stone who had complained

about his umbrellas got up and ran, while other umbrellas blossomed in the small crowd. The woman holding the umbrella over the senator stayed rigidly in place, while he tried to go on. She was getting soaked, as he was from about his chest down.

Stone, Jenna, and Eggers were unable to suppress laughter, while Slade soldiered on, glowering at them.

"I'm informed that the rain will pass shortly!" he shouted.

Stone shouted back, "Who informed you of that? God?"

A very wet man in a seersucker suit ran up to Stone. "Please, let's maintain decorum!"

"This is indecorous weather!" Stone shouted back.

"You think this is indecorous?" Slade yelled, joining the conversation. "Wait until I slap you silly!"

"I'm waiting," Stone yelled back. "Try it!"

Slade grabbed the microphone, turned, and walked up the steps to the porch of the building, followed by the woman with the umbrella, trying desperately to keep up with him. "Now," he said, "with a little shelter, I believe I can continue."

"The rest of us don't have any shelter!" Stone shouted.

The audience, such as it was, scattered to the winds, seeking shelter.

Then there was a flash of light from the audio-system box, and Slade screamed and dropped the microphone.

"God is calling again," Stone yelled. "A new message!"

A man in a blue suit appeared from inside the building with a velvet box and a robe slung over an arm. "Here's your degree!" he shouted. "And your robes. Would you like me to help you on with them?"

A woman appeared and offered Slade his Stetson, which he jammed onto his head.

"And now you've been handed your hat!" Stone shouted. "That's your cue for your exit!"

Slade stalked off toward the parking lot, while the woman with the umbrella tried to follow.

Egger and Jenna were helpless with laughter, and Stone found it infectious. He sat down and laughed with them. Some minutes passed, then a ray of sunshine beat down on them and the rain stopped, as if turned off by a spigot in the sky. Gradually, the three of them gained control of themselves.

"What now?" Stone asked.

"Let's hunt him down and throw stones at him," Jenna suggested.

"I've no wish," Eggers said, "to spend the night in the Hearthrug jail. Suggest something else."

"It's brown whiskey weather," Stone said. "Let's go home and drink some."

"Now, that's what I call a suggestion," Eggers said.

They all stood up. Jenna said, "There must be something else we can do to humiliate Wallace."

Then, across the lawn, Harley Quince stepped through a hedge in his black Stetson, wearing a black rubber cape.

Stone looked at him. "My best guess on what's under the cape is a shotgun. What's yours?"

"I'll buy that," Eggers said. "Let's get the hell out of here."

They ran for Jenna's car. They had to wade the last twenty feet, as the car park had become a puddle. Stone got the wet umbrellas into the rear compartment, then started the car. "Does this thing have four-wheel drive?" he asked.

"I think so," Jenna said.

"I guess we're about to find out," Eggers said from the rear seat.

Stone put the car in gear, tapped the accelerator, and let the car move itself through a huge puddle, which seemed to be about up to the wheel hubs now.

From somewhere behind them, they heard a motorcycle crank up noisily.

"I guess we're about to find out, too, how a BMW motorcycle does in these conditions." Stone steered for the main gate and went just a little faster.

"Here he comes," Eggers said, looking rearward.

Stone checked the rearview mirror and saw Quince, his legs spread out, plowing through the water. "Oh, shit," he said. "We should have come armed."

"Well," Jenna said, "I'd rather be in jail than dead."

"I'm afraid it's too late to reconsider," Eggers said. "Can you paddle faster, Stone?"

"I'm paddling as fast as I can," Stone said. "How's Quince doing?"

"Ha!" Eggers shouted. "He just took a spill."

Then they were in shallower water, then on a reasonably dry road that ran through the main gate. A moment later, they were on the road and headed back to Washington.

49

Back at his Washington house, Eggers resumed his duties as cook and made a big salad for lunch. They were seated at the kitchen table, having polished off the salad, when Jenna spoke up.

"I think we're in big trouble," she said.

"Oh?" Stone said. "Why?"

"Well, we've made Wallace volcanically angry, and we've pissed off Harley pretty good, too. Neither of them behaves rationally when angry. I mean, we've just confirmed to the public what some of them may have already suspected: that Wallace is an asshole."

"I can't argue that point," Stone said.

"In public," Jenna said. "In public is bad angry. I know what he's like when he's angry in private, and I have the scars to prove it. But public humiliation sets off a tidal wave of rage in Wallace, and he will do anything—**anything**—for revenge against those he holds responsible for his humiliation. And there we were, in the audience, a few yards away from where Wallace was revealing his true nature to everybody within earshot at the Hearthrug Bible College, shouting at him and holding him up to ridicule."

Everybody was quiet for a moment, then Eggers said, "I'd better trot out the shotguns."

"Trot out everything you've got," Stone said, reaching for his phone and calling the team leader from Strategic Services.

"Yes?"

"It's Stone. How many men have you got on hand right now?"

"Two," the man said, "and I'm one of them. The rest have gone in search of lunch, and cell service is spotty around here. I'll try my radio."

"You do that. And get everybody to the Eggers house armed to the teeth. We're expecting trouble." He hung up.

"It won't happen immediately," Jenna said.

"That's good news," Stone said, "but why not?"

"Because Wallace is a coward, and he won't come after us with only Harley to help him. He will amass his forces."

"Well, who the hell is he going to amass in rural Connecticut?"

"Those folks from the Bible college, maybe," she said.

"They're lambs. They're not violent people."

"You didn't read that bulletin board on the way to the speech area. There were posts for things like raids on abortion clinics, and reprints of right-wing essays on hate, and articles about having their guns confiscated by the government. I wouldn't be surprised if those folks had an arsenal in a cellar somewhere on campus."

"Maybe we'd better get out of here and go back to New York," Eggers said, "or to my house in Greenwich."

"I'd like to hear what our security guy says. We shouldn't go off half-cocked," Stone said.

"Okay," Eggers said, "I'll give the guy five minutes to convince me, before I take it on the lam."

As he spoke, a Range Rover drove up, parked in front of the house, and the Strategic Services team leader, Ken, got out.

"Here he comes," Stone said.

"Alone," Eggers pointed out.

"He said everybody's at lunch, and he can't reach them on a cell phone."

"Does he have a radio?"

"He said he'd try that."

"We're right on the village green here," Eggers said, "and it's the highest point around. If he's going to find any kind of reception, he'll find it here."

Ken walked into the house without knocking. "Hello?"

"In the kitchen," Stone said.

The man walked into the kitchen and looked around. "What's with the shotguns?" he asked.

"We're expecting some kind of invasion," Stone said.

"On what evidence?"

"On the evidence of Jenna's hunch."

"You get strong hunches, do you, Jenna?"

"Only about Wallace Slade, and my hunch is: he's coming for us."

"When?"

"Just as soon as he can raise a mob and find a rope."

Ken looked at Stone. "You're taking this seriously, then?"

"She knows Slade better than anybody else here, including you," Stone replied. "I think it would be stupid to do anything but believe her and get ready for an assault."

"Okay. I'd better try my radio again," Ken said, then unsheathed it. "Mayday, Mayday, Mayday," he said into the radio.

"Who's calling Mayday?" somebody responded.

"It's Ken. Where are you, and how many?"

"We're at a restaurant in Washington Depot."

"How many?"

"Two."

"Where's everybody else?"

"I don't know. They didn't want to wait for a table here."

"Assemble everybody you can find, meet at the Eggers house, and bring weapons and body armor, **stat**!"

"You think the villagers are going to torch the house?"

"I think you had better move your ass," Ken said. "Don't finish your lunch."

"Wilco. We'll search the area for the others. The weapons and armor are in the van, and we're in the Range Rover."

Ken put down the radio. "Well, shit. What the hell happened that would make Slade attack us?"

"Ah, well," Stone said. "We were not a very good audience for his acceptance speech."

"How not very good?"

"Pretty bad. We humiliated the guy."

"You poked the pig, huh?"

"That's about the size of it."

"Let me give you some advice," Ken said.

"Never poke the pig?"

"That's it."

50

Stone rapped on the table for attention. "Listen to me," he said.

Everybody quieted down. "When that van gets here, and we're all armed, we have to be careful what weapons we choose. Ken, what's in the van?"

"Heckler & Koch light machine guns, assault rifles, riot guns—they're 12-gauge shotguns with 24½-inch barrels, typically used by police for riot control, and 9mm Beretta semiautomatic pistols, the standard sidearms for U.S. troops. Also, several thousand rounds of ammo, to cover all the types."

"What kind of shotgun shells?"

"Buckshot and birdshot, number nine."

"All right. We can't get into a firefight using

hard ammo: we'd be firing live rounds into houses, and there's a private school across the road called the Frederick Gunn School. We'd have a lot of collateral damage, and nobody's going to be interested in why."

"What do you suggest?" Ken asked.

"I say we use the riot guns with birdshot loads, the lightest weapons we have. They'll make lots of noise, but they're not going to penetrate the walls of buildings some distance away and kill the inhabitants."

"That makes sense," Ken said.

"Do you think Wallace will be so restrained?" Jenna asked. "My guess is he won't be as discriminating as you are. He'll use whatever he can get his hands on, and I bet that will mean assault weapons."

"We can't let ourselves be responsible for Slade's bad decisions," Stone replied. "We're going to have to be able to prove to whatever police turn up that we were acting in self-defense and not trying to kill anybody. Also, when we fire, we should fire at their feet, so that we don't blow anybody away. Cripple them, but don't kill them. If somebody takes a round of birdshot in his shin, he's not going to be thinking about killing us after that."

"Let's not be overcautious while they're firing hard rounds at us," Eggers said.

"Overcautious is exactly what we have to be,"

Stone said. "Ken, is there any body armor in that van?"

"A dozen suits," he replied. "None of them small enough for Jenna."

"She can wear baggy armor if it will save her life. Speaking of the van, where the hell is it?"

Ken peered out a window. "Coming down Kirby Road," he said, "and fast."

"Do you see any opposition yet?"

Ken checked again, this time with binoculars. "No."

"Then let's get that van unloaded, but only shotguns and birdshot. Leave the heavy stuff for the cops to discover when they search the van—all they'll find is proof of our benign intentions."

"Line up," Ken said. "Let's do a kind of bucket brigade. I'll choose the weapons. The rest of you just hand them into the kitchen."

Ken went out to meet the van and motioned it as close to the front door as he could get it. It stopped, and Ken opened the sliding doors, barking orders at the men inside. Ten minutes later there was a pile of weapons and ammo on the entrance hall floor, and people were figuring out how to wear the body armor.

"I was wrong," Ken said, holding up a suit. "We have one woman-sized suit." He helped Jenna into it.

Stone looked out the window and saw three

vans turn onto their street. "Here they come," he said. "And remember, don't let anybody get behind the house. We don't have enough people to defend the whole perimeter, we just want to scare them off. And don't shoot out their tires; that would slow them in running away."

"Can you use this?" Ken asked, holding up a bullhorn.

"Perfect," Stone said. "They can't misunderstand our intentions if we're shouting at them for the neighbors to hear."

Ken ran out the door, and Stone watched as he locked up the van and returned to the house. "We don't want them to use our own weapons against us," he said.

They watched as Wallace Slade got out of a van and marched to about fifty feet from the house, holding an assault rifle in one hand and his own bullhorn in the other.

"You in there!" he roared over the bullhorn. "Come out of there with your hands up and face the people's justice!"

Stone aimed a round about three feet short of Slade's feet and fired. The pellets ricocheted into his ankles, and he did a little dance for them, using a lot of language that Bible students would be unaccustomed to hearing.

"Get out of here, Wallace!" Stone shouted over his bullhorn, "and take those innocent people with you, before you get them hurt!"

Wallace dropped his assault weapon and bull-horn and limped as fast as he could back toward his van. The door opened and he dove inside, then, to Stone's surprise, all three vans made U-turns and sped back up the street.

"Do you think they'll be back?" Stone asked.

"If they do come back," Jenna said, "Wallace won't be leading them."

51

Time for Stone to make another speech. "Now we have to get out of Connecticut," he said.

"Where to?" Jenna asked.

"My house in New York."

"Just when we've got them on the run?"

"They'll only be on the run until Wallace convinces them they should come back. As soon as he's tweezed the birdshot out of his ankles, he'll start in on them. Once he can tap-dance again, they'll believe they can't get hurt."

"Look at it this way," Eggers said. "There's no downside to getting out of here and heading to . . . somewhere else. If they come over all brave, then they can shoot up Stone's house instead of mine."

"What they don't know," Stone said, "is my house is pretty much bulletproof."

"Why?" someone asked.

"Because some years ago, when I was doing some consulting for the CIA, they became concerned for my safety. I moved out for a couple of weeks, and they took off the siding, installed a layer of half-inch-steel plating, then replaced the siding, along with new windows with armored glass."

"I want to go there," Jenna said, and no one disagreed with her.

———

Three hours later, Stone opened the garage door to the house next door to his, and drove in, followed by a vanload of Strategic Services agents. The door closed behind them. Stone entered the security code at the door to the house and let everybody inside.

"I know this place," Ken said. Then he started issuing instructions as to where his agents should be.

Stone and Jenna excused themselves until dinnertime, went upstairs, and flung themselves at each other.

"This is why you wanted to come back here," Jenna said, after the first round.

"It's important for your peace of mind that you be periodically well-fucked," Stone replied.

"Well said. Can we do it again, please?"

"Just take deep breaths and give me a few minutes," Stone said. He got into the shower, shaved, and then returned for round two and was enthusiastically received at the bell.

A few minutes later, Bob Cantor was on the phone. "Sorry to disturb you."

"I'm not disturbed."

"I wanted you to know that I checked out the whole-house systems, and everything is intact, and there are no bugs anywhere. This is a first for you, Stone."

"It is, and good to know. Thanks."

"Who was that?" Jenna asked.

"That was my security guy," he said. "He says it's all right for you to be fucked again, without fear of being disturbed."

"He's not going to get an argument from me," she said, reaching for him.

———

Lying there a while later, panting and sweating, Stone heard the house phone go off. "Yes?"

"It's Joan. I just wanted you to know that there are at least two SWAT teams roaming the house, armed with shotguns. Shall I retrieve my .45 from my desk drawer?"

"No, they're here at my invitation, and they've promised not to shoot you."

"I wanted to be of help."

"Oh, good."

"Are the three vanloads of people with very short haircuts, who are driving around the block repeatedly, included in that invitation?"

"Funny you should mention that." Stone sat up on one elbow. "All right," he said, "go get your .45. Then get back to your apartment and lock down. You're outgunned."

"Yes, boss."

Stone called Ken on his cell phone.

"Yes, sir?"

"Have you taken note of the three vanloads of Bible students circling the block?"

"Yes, sir. We'll allow them the first move, then we'll greet them more seriously."

"Before they make their move, call Dino Bacchetti and tell him we're under threat. Let's let the NYPD do as much of our work as possible."

"Yes, sir."

"Who is it this time?" Jenna asked.

"Bible students," Stone replied. "Who else?"

"Shall we greet them as we are, or is clothing in order?"

Stone ran a hand down her body. "Regretfully, clothing is in order. Do you still have the armored suit?"

"No. You said the house would take care of us."

"And it will," Stone said, heading for a shotgun. He could hear squad-car whoopers in the distance.

———

He found Ken in Joan's office, staring out the front door. "What's going on?"

"I'm just watching the NYPD doing my job for me. This is fun."

Stone joined him and saw the Bible students assuming the position against their vans and cops tossing various weapons into the trunks of police cruisers. "It's nice to be able to lead the flock to a place where they can be safely sheared of their hardware. Have you seen the goon senator anywhere?"

"Apparently, neither he nor Mr. Quince made the trip down—or if they did, they hotfooted it out of here when they heard the cops coming."

"I'd be interested to know if they make bail, and how much," Stone said.

"I'll get somebody down to the court," Ken replied.

"Somebody who can argue against bail. Do you know Herbert Fisher?"

"I do."

"Him."

52

Herbie Fisher had been alerted, so Stone and Ken, the detail commander, took a break in Stone's office, where the fruits of Kentucky were tasted. After Ken left, Stone was still, unaccountably, taking deep breaths. "I'm feeling a little bushed," he admitted to himself.

Then his chin sagged to his chest, and a moment later, he slid from the chair and onto the carpet with a deep sigh.

He was not unconscious, he reflected, but neither did he seem to be capable of conscious movement or even of planning such. It wasn't unpleasant, as long as he didn't think about it. He tried to look around the room, but his vision, though working, was incapable of swiveling, zooming, or fixing upon an object for very long before it began to wander.

He was appreciating the soft texture of the hand-woven Persian carpet upon which his cheek rested when something filled most of his field of vision. When he thought about it for a time, he decided it was a boot of western origin.

"He's out," a not unfamiliar voice said.

"His eyes are open," an even less unfamiliar voice replied.

"It's the gas," Voice One said. "It affects different people in different ways."

"Will it kill him?" Voice Two asked.

"To be determined."

Stone found this exchange disturbing. Who were they talking about? Certainly not him; he didn't feel even a little deceased. In fact, he felt buoyant, perfectly contented. Well, he reflected after a moment, not perfectly so. In fact, he seemed, though comfortable, paralyzed, sort of. He tried wiggling a toe. That seemed to work, though he was unable to confirm that by any available means, so he wiggled a finger. That worked, though he wasn't sure which finger.

"You want me to off him?" Voice One asked.

"Not yet," Voice Two said. "I want to have a good look around this house first. See if there's anything I'd like to steal or, if necessary, buy from his estate. And I want to leave the medical examiner a fresh corpse."

"I'll follow you," Voice One said, and the two seemed to drift away.

Fresh corpse? Stone thought. That meant recently dead, didn't it? And they seemed to be referring to him. It occurred to him that he might not be taking his position seriously enough. He tried wiggling all his fingers at once. Ten working fingers, five on each hand. He tried getting a palm-down hand under his face, and then to right himself. That worked long enough to get an elbow under his body, then lean on it. His field of vision was now occupied by a telephone on the coffee table. It seemed to be within his grasp, if he could reach.

He made a monumental attempt to grab the phone and missed.

Wait a minute, he thought. There was a better solution to this problem if he could just remember what it was. He devoted himself to that for a moment. "Cell," he said. He managed to roll onto his back and grope for the scabbard that held his iPhone. A moment later, it was in his hand. Then he dropped it, and he couldn't figure out where.

Then the phone on the coffee table spoke to him. "Boss?" it said.

"Boss," he repeated.

"Is that you?"

"Boss."

"What's wrong?"

"Gas."

"I'll get you something for that," she said. "Can you hang on for a minute?"

"NO!"

"You sound funny," she said.

"Yes."

"I'm coming down there."

"No."

"Why not?"

"Gas."

"Have we got a gas leak?"

"No. Call Dino." He fell back onto the floor, exhausted by his efforts. What he needed was a nap.

"I like those paintings," Voice Two suddenly said. Stone had enough consciousness to know not to move. "I'll bet there are more," Two said. "They're by his mother."

"Why does that matter?" Voice One said.

"I don't know, it just does."

"Can we get the paintings into the van?"

"Yeah, and him, too."

"He's not a lightweight, you know."

"That's why you're going to do all the work, Harley."

The name Harley got through the fog to Stone's ear. It made him feel . . . What was the word? Revulsion.

"Was he lying like that when we left?" Slade said.

"He probably twitched a little. They do that sometimes."

"Maybe you should bind him before we move him," Slade said.

"Bind him with what?"

Oh, no, Stone thought. Not duct tape.

"Duct tape," Slade said. "Find some."

Stone did not like duct tape. He had had an unpleasant encounter with it once before, and he didn't want to repeat the experience. He looked up through the glass-topped coffee table and saw something sharp: a letter opener, made from an old hunting knife. He had bought it in a thrift shop somewhere. He began to think about how to get a hand on it.

53

The two men left, in pursuit of duct tape. Stone managed to roll on his side and fling an arm onto the coffee table. A moment later, he had the letter opener in his hand, before rolling onto his back again.

"Here's some duct tape," Harley called from the supply room.

"Well, take it to Barrington," Slade said.

There was some rustling from the supply room; probably Harley getting a new box of duct tape open. Stone had a thing about leaving the stuff lying around, ever since his previous experience with it, so Joan kept it out of his sight.

Harley arrived with a gas mask around his face and the duct tape in hand and tried to move the inert Stone away from the coffee table. Finally, he succeeded, and wrapped duct tape around Stone's ankles, binding them together. "You got a knife?" he asked.

"No," Slade replied from still inside the supply room, "but if you do it right, you can just tear the tape with your fingers."

Harley made some grunting noises, and apparently succeeded in tearing the tape. "There." He moved up Stone's body to tape his hands.

Then, a voice from the air: "Stone, I can't find what I'm looking for. Have you got anything in your bathroom for gas?"

"NO!" Stone yelled, and with all the strength and coordination he could muster, he reached up and stabbed Harley Quince in his genitals. It was a near miss, and he plunged the blade into the man's upper thigh.

Quince let out something between a yell and a scream. "Goddamnit! He stabbed me!"

"You stupid little shit," Slade said conversationally. "He's unconscious, he can't stab anybody."

Quince jumped backward, leaving the old knife in Stone's hand; his heel caught in Stone's taped ankles, and he fell heavily, his head striking a bronze sculpture of a small bear behind him.

"Stone?" Joan's voice said. "Are you in difficulties?"

"YES!" Stone yelled back.

"Harley?" Slade said. "What's the matter with you? What did you say?"

Stone managed to get his ankles in range and began sawing at the duct tape, but the blade was dull, and he was still weak.

"Stone?" Joan asked.

"Shut up, you stupid bitch"—Slade shouted as he walked into the room—"or I'll shoot you, too!"

"HELP!" Stone shouted.

"Coming!" Joan yelled back.

Stone's tongue and lips were working now. "Better not shoot," he said. "Armed men."

Slade came toward him. "Harley? What's the matter with you?"

"No dick," Stone said helpfully.

Slade stood over Quince and looked down at him. "You're bleeding like a stuck pig," he said, maneuvering to keep his boots out of the pool of blood that was gathering.

"Nine-one-one," Harley said. "Quick!"

"Did that bastard stab you in the dick?"

"Thigh," Harley replied, sounding weaker.

"Ah," Slade said. "It appears he nicked an artery, Harley. Nine-one-one won't help." He pulled off his necktie, wrapped it around Harley's leg, and tied it off.

Stone felt a draft of fresh air, reviving him further. Someone had opened the door to the garage. He heard the slide of a pistol racking.

"Don't shoot, Wallace," Stone said.

A pistol roared, and Stone flinched in anticipation. It roared again.

Slade fell across the glass coffee table, shattering it.

"Joan?" Stone said.

"I got the son of a bitch," she said.

"Did you shoot him in the head?"

"I don't think so."

"Why not?" Stone demanded.

"I was aiming at his chest. That's what you do at the range."

"Give me your pistol, and I'll shoot him in the head," Stone said. He heard himself and couldn't believe he'd said that.

"Are you speaking as my lawyer?" she asked.

"Not exactly. What's he doing?"

"He's clutching his chest and bleeding," she replied.

"I guess that's good enough," Stone said. "Did you call nine-one-one?"

"Nope. In all the excitement, I forgot."

"Now would be a good time," Stone said. "Then Dino. Dino prefers you to call nine-one-one first, then him."

Joan sat down in Stone's usual chair and picked up the phone. "What do I say?"

"Say 'intruder shot, also his accomplice. Send two ambulances.'"

Joan did as he said, then dialed another number and handed the phone to Stone. "You explain it to Dino."

54

Stone got hold of the phone. "Dino?"

"Yeah, what's up?"

Stone thought about it and drew a blank. "I can't remember."

"What's the matter with you, Stone?"

Stone remembered. "Gas."

"Well, fart, and it'll go away."

"Not that gas."

"You mean you've been gassed?"

Thank God, Stone thought. That's the word I've been trying to remember. "Gassed," he said with some satisfaction.

"Who gassed you?"

"Senator."

Joan grabbed the phone. "Dino, for Christ's sake, two people are shot and one is gassed. I called nine-one-one, but I don't think they believed me."

"Is Stone shot?"

"No, just gassed."

"I'll call nine-one-one," Dino said. "They'll listen to me." He hung up.

"Dino's on it," Joan said. "Finally."

Stone lay on his back, sucking in breaths. He looked at where the coffee table had stood and saw a white Stetson with drops of blood on it. "Did you shoot him in the head?" he asked Joan.

"No, in the upper chest. Looks like it went through and through."

"Why didn't you shoot him in the head?"

"Don't start that again!"

"Start what?"

There was a banging on the door, and Joan went to answer it. Two teams of EMTs barged in. "Which one's worse?" one of them asked Stone.

"I dunno. Take your pick."

"I've got a bleeder over here," the EMT said. "Gimme a tourniquet."

"There's a nice necktie on it," Stone said.

"Who is this guy?" he asked Joan, pointing to Stone. "Did you shoot him?"

"He is unshot," Joan said.

"What's wrong with him?"

"Gas."

"I never got a call for gas," he said, poking at Stone.

"He's **been** gassed," she said.

"What kind of gas?"

"I don't know. They brought it with them," she said, holding up the gas mask that hung around Slade's neck.

"What a mess!" the man said, cutting off the gas mask with scissors.

"Police!" somebody yelled.

"And about fucking time," Joan said to Dino.

"Don't start with me, Joan," Dino said. "Where's Stone?"

"You see all that broken glass?"

"Yeah."

"He's underneath it."

"I already checked him out," the EMT said, buckling Slade onto a stretcher. "He's okay, except for the gas."

"Gas, again," Dino said.

"Where are you taking me?" Slade asked weakly.

"Bellevue," the man said.

"No you are not!" Slade replied. "You are taking me to New York Hospital, and I want you to call Dr. Stanley Weinberg, the chief of surgery, and tell him I'm on the way."

"I'm not your social secretary, pal," the EMT said, picking his way through the glass.

"You're not going to be anything in an hour," Slade said, "if you don't call Weinberg." Then he fainted.

"Thank God, he's out," the EMT said. "I guess

we'd better go to the New York Hospital trauma center. It's just as close."

"I want to go to Lenox Hill Hospital," Stone said. "I'm known there."

"Oh, well, sure. Can I mix you a martini on the way?"

"Bourbon," Stone said. "Knob Creek, rocks."

"You'd better deliver them as requested," Joan said. "Otherwise, I'll never hear the end of it."

"What about the bleeder? What do we do with him?"

"Anything you like," Joan replied.

The next team came after Stone. "Stop!" Stone said, suddenly lucid. "All I need is oxygen. I've been gassed."

The EMT looked at Joan. "Well?"

"Give him oxygen, dummy! He's been gassed!"

They sat Stone up in a wing chair and got an oxygen mask on him. Joan poured him a Knob Creek on the rocks and handed it to him.

"Here," she said, "do yourself some good."

Stone lifted his mask and took a big swig. "Did they leave without me?" he asked.

"Yeah," Joan replied, "they said you were too much trouble."

"Dino, does the NYPD have a gas squad? Sort of like the bomb squad?"

Joan handed Dino a Scotch. "Nobody's ever asked for a gas squad," he said, taking a pull on his drink. "I'll look into that."

"Never mind," Stone said, shucking off his mask. "I feel normal now."

"Uh-oh," Dino said. "Where's Jenna?"

"Jenna who?"

"Wallace Slade's ex?"

"She's around here somewhere," Stone replied.

Joan got up. "She must have taken shelter somewhere. I'll root her out."

"Who shot Slade?" Dino asked.

"Joan did."

"Why didn't she shoot him in the head?"

55

Fred and Helene had mopped and cleaned all the relevant parts of Stone's study, and Joan had ordered a new coffee-table top from a glass shop. Stone and Dino had helped by having a second drink.

Dino's phone rang. "Bacchetti. Yeah. Yeah? Too bad. Keep me posted." He hung up.

"Well?" Stone asked.

"Okay, Wallace Slade had his wound cleaned and stitched, and is demanding to be released."

"Jesus, he had a shoulder wound!"

"No, he had a shoulder through-and-through. The bullet is probably around here somewhere." He glanced about him but didn't move.

"It's not in the Scotch bottle," Joan said. "Nor,

come to that, the bourbon bottle. A thorough search of both has been made."

"It'll turn up when my guys get around to it. There are a lot of new cases today."

"Most of them in this room," Joan said.

"Come on, Joan," Stone said, "why aren't you drinking?"

"Well, **somebody's** got to remain conscious around here."

"There's nothing in the air but air," Stone said, taking a couple of deep breaths. "I've tested it personally."

"Give Fred and Helene a two-hundred-dollar bonus for the cleanup."

"Already done, but I gave them three hundred each. I don't think Quince had any blood left in him."

"Oh, I forgot about Quince," Dino said. "He survived, after many transfusions."

"Pity," Stone said. "Where's Jenna?"

"She slept through everything," Joan said. "In fact, she's still sleeping."

"The woman is a heroic sleeper," Stone replied. "Don't wake her."

"Maybe we can get out of here and go to Clarke's, for some dinner, while she's still out," Dino said.

"Right," Stone said, getting to his feet. "We'll bring her a steak in a bag." He teetered a bit. "Gotta get my land legs back," he said.

"Do it in my car," Dino said, heading for the door.

———

They skipped the bar, went straight to their table, and ordered steaks. "Dino, did your people figure out what kind of gas they used?"

"Nah, the gas squad said there was no label on the bottles."

"I thought you said you don't have a gas squad."

"I do now," Dino said. "But like I said, there was no label on the bottles."

"Can't the gas squad analyze it?"

"They're not the chemistry squad," Dino said. "They're sending it out for that."

Jenna walked up to their table. "You left me," she said accusingly.

"You were unconscious," Stone said.

"We ordered you a steak in a bag," Dino said.

Jenna hipped Stone over a few inches. "Well, tell them to shake it out of the bag."

Dino grabbed a passing waiter and issued the instructions.

"Anything else disturbing you?" Stone asked. "You don't look happy."

"Why didn't Joan shoot Wallace in the head?"

"You'll have to consult Joan on that," he replied. "I think it's hard to shoot somebody in the head with a .45."

"Messy, too," Dino said.

"I would have found it a snap," Jenna said.

"Next time we need somebody shot in the head, we'll wake you," Stone said.

"Please."

"Did somebody tell you Wallace isn't dead?"

"I got that."

"And Quince survived," Stone said.

"Now that is unconscionable," Jenna said. "I heard you were trying to geld him."

"I missed. I was trying for the whole package. He must have flinched or something, but I did nick an artery, I forget which one. Fred and Helene recovered a bucketful of blood. Why are you looking so dour?" he asked.

"They'll come for me again," Jenna replied. "Didn't I explain that to you?"

"I guess I didn't . . ."

"Believe me?"

"Uh . . ."

"Take me seriously? After being married to Wallace, I'm weary of not being taken seriously."

"Are you taking yourself seriously?" Stone asked.

"What do you mean?"

"I mean you left the house alone and went out into the street, looking for a cab, in utter disregard of your own safety."

"Well, it's **my** safety! I'll disregard it if I like!"

"But I can't?"

"Exactly."

Their steaks came while Stone was trying to think of a retort, and he was spared. "You can't argue with an angry woman," he muttered.

"You can argue with one," Dino said. "You just can't win."

56

Harley Quince awoke in a hospital room. A man in an adjacent bed seemed to have wakened him merely by staring at him. "Senator?" he guessed.

Wallace Slade's right shoulder was bandaged, and his arm in a sling. "Asshole," he said.

Harley shifted in his bed a little to get a better view. "What did you call me?"

"Asshole."

"Where do you come off . . ."

"You allowed that . . . **female** person to shoot me."

Harley raised his bed up. "I was pretty busy for a while, you may recall."

"**I** saved **your** life," Slade said. "I applied a tourniquet to your leg."

"Thank you very much," Harley said. "I'm very grateful . . ."

"Asshole."

"Senator, if you say that to me again, I'm going to find a sharp instrument and cut your throat."

"I apologize."

"That's better. What do you want me to do?"

"I want the two of us to get out of these beds, go to Barrington's house, and kill Jenna. You can cut her up, if you like. I'll hold her down."

"Why in Barrington's house? It's a fortress."

"Because that's where she is. If we allow her to leave, we won't know where she is."

"You have a point," Harley said. "What about our injuries? I've just had four hours of surgery to repair the artery."

"I talked with the doctor about that. He says the artery is stronger now than before, because of the kind of repair he made." This was a lie.

"He said that, really?"

"Ask him yourself."

"He told me when he examined me that he was leaving today on a three-week vacation to the islands."

"Take my word for what he said."

"What about your arm?"

"It's not my arm, it's my shoulder. It's a through-and-through wound, through the fleshypart."

"Do you feel like going out and killing her right now?"

"Oh, yes. Nothing would heal me faster."

"Let's give it until tomorrow, when the pain-killer has worn off, and see then."

"Well, take more painkiller," Slade replied.

"I'm too tired to do it right now."

"Okay, we'll get a few nights' sleep, then we'll kill her." He thought about it a little more. "I want to kill the bitch that shot me, too."

"We'll talk about it tomorrow," Harley said, drifting off.

That night, Jenna seemed to melt into Stone's arms. "I'm so sorry about the way I've been behaving," she said, kissing Stone in a very nice place.

"It's all right. You've been under a lot of pressure," Stone said.

"Doing this makes me feel more relaxed," she said, pausing only long enough to speak.

"Well, I certainly want you to be relaxed," Stone panted.

_____

In the morning, when they were having breakfast in bed, Jenna said, "May I have a gun, please?"

"Huh?"

"A gun. I'd feel safer."

"Jenna, I've explained to you about the New York City laws on that subject."

"Oh, not to go out with. Just for around the house."

"Ah, an around-the-house gun."

"Yes."

"I'll see what I can find for you."

He went to his safe and found the little KelTec .380, the one with the silencer. Lance Cabot had given it to him when they had visited the CIA's Farm, their training center, but he had never fired it. He took it to her with a box of ammo and a pair of magazines, then showed her how to load the cartridges and to reload after emptying a magazine. Jenna had clearly spent some time around weapons, and he felt better about arming her.

"But remember," he said, "you can't take it out of the house. If you were found by a cop to be armed, not even Dino could keep you out of jail."

"Don't worry, I've no wish to go to jail. But if I ever find myself facing Wallace again, I want to be ready."

"Fair enough, but I think Wallace's wound is going to keep him in the hospital for a couple of weeks."

"What about Harley's wound?"

"He won't be going anywhere for a while, except in a wheelchair."

"What's Dino charging them with?"

"Well, that's kind of a problem. Wallace has lawyered up, and so has Harley. They might walk, eventually."

Jenna nodded. "I'm not surprised."

"I think you should stay with me until that issue is resolved," Stone said.

"Perhaps I'll do that," she said. "If you'll have me."

"Having you is my favorite thing," Stone said.

———

Three days later, Senator Wallace Slade lay back in his hospital bed and ran his fingers through the hair of the young lady in a candy-striper's uniform whose head was in his lap. She had been a special order from a local madam of his acquaintance. He liked the uniform.

Having finished her work, she brushed the wrinkles out of her clothes. "You have something for me?"

"Of course, baby. You have something else for me, too, don't you?"

She held up a bottle of pills. "Super-duper pain medication," she said. "And with a kick, too."

He peeled off some hundreds and took the pills.

"Tomorrow?" she asked.

"Sweetheart, I'll be gone from here tomorrow."

"Keep in touch," she said, and left the room.

Harley spoke from the other bed. "Some for me, too?" he asked.

"Enough to keep you floating on air," Slade replied. "Tomorrow's the day. You up for it?"

"I will be," Harley said. "I may need a cane—something sturdy, that I can weaponize."

"I know where we can get something special for you. We'll have a weapons delivery first thing in the morning."

———

Stone called Mike Freeman. "Good morning."

"How are things?" Mike asked.

"It's time for your people to be called off," Stone said. "Wallace and his acolyte are disabled, and it's been very peaceful all week. And you're making too much money."

"Okay. I'll pull everybody off the job," Mike said. "You have enough of your own firepower to handle emergencies, right?"

"Yes, and I've got Joan and Fred, too."

"You tell those two that if they ever want out, I've got jobs waiting for them at Strategic Services."

"I'll tell them no such thing, and don't you, either!" Stone hung up.

Dino called. "Dinner tonight? Patroon?"

"You're on. Seven o'clock?"

"Right." Dino hung up.

———

Late in the day, someone knocked lightly on the door of Wallace Slade's room. "Come!" he shouted.

The door opened and a suitcase on wheels entered, followed closely by a middle-aged woman in dowdy clothes. "Hey there, Senator," she said. "Delivery for you." She pointed at the suitcase.

"Just put it on the bed," he said.

With some effort, she managed it, and he unzipped the suitcase.

Harley hobbled over and looked into the case. "Ahh," he said.

"Me, too," Wallace replied. He took an envelope from a bedside drawer and handed it to her. "Tell him thanks, from me," he said.

She gave him a little salute and left, closing the door behind her.

58

Stone was awakened by the sound of his doorbell ringing. He checked his bedside clock: eight o'clock. Joan wouldn't be in yet. He pressed the intercom button, which turned on a camera, too. "Yes?"

"FedEx delivery," a voice said. Stone could see, from slightly above, a baseball cap that had the FedEx logo on it. "You need a signature?"

"No, but I can't leave it on the doorstep, either."

"I'll buzz you in. Just leave it inside the door, on the table."

"Right."

Stone pressed the correct button to open the door. When he checked the camera again, the FedEx guy was gone. Stone was too sleepy to go downstairs and open the package. He rolled over and went back to sleep. Jenna slept soundly beside him.

———

Slade and Quince were inside the door before closing it, and so was Slade's suitcase. They opened it and began assembling weapons.

Quince held up a cane. "I like it," he said. "I can rap somebody with the hand grip and hit 'em hard with the weighted tip. Where to?"

"He sounded sleepy to me, so I'm going to leave him in peace upstairs. Let's go to the office. I want to deal with that secretary when she comes to work." They found their way to Stone's office and made themselves comfortable there. Each of them had a silenced 9mm handgun that had been loaded and wiped clean, inside and out. Each wore latex gloves.

"How do you want to do this?" Harley asked.

"One at a time," Wallace replied. "We'll take the secretary and the butler guy down here, then go upstairs and take Barrington and my bitch. If we get lucky, I'd like to take them while they're fucking."

Harley laughed. "And what shall I do?"

"Watch my back. Use your cane freely."

———

Joan made a deposit at the bank as soon as it opened, then started for Stone's house, less than two blocks away.

———

"What's the holdup?" Quince asked. "It's a little after nine o'clock."

"Relax. Maybe she made a stop on the way to work."

"Whatever you say."

"What about the butler?"

"I saw him leave the house right before you got here. He got a cab somewhere."

Joan turned the corner. As she did, she saw something in the block that shouldn't have been there. All the cars normally parked on the downtown side of the street should have moved, for the sake of alternate-side parking, which the residents adhered to for street cleaning. But today there was a single car parked there, where it shouldn't be: a Lincoln Town Car, one she didn't know. She reached into her handbag.

———

Upstairs, Stone got out of the shower and put on a terry-cloth robe. Then from downstairs came a loud noise, like the slamming of a heavy door. Stone stopped in his tracks: nobody in his household slammed doors. He went to his dressing room and removed his Colt Government .380

from the shoulder holster that hung on a hook with his trousers. He checked the weapon, worked the action, set the safety, then stuck a spare magazine into the left pocket of the robe and walked, barefoot, to the head of the stairs, where he stopped and listened. He heard a loud crash, one he had heard before and recently: glass breaking. The new glass for his coffee table had been delivered the afternoon before, and someone had broken it already. He started down the stairs at a trot, his hand in his robe pocket, on the .380.

At the foot of the stairs, he stopped and listened again. Dead silence. This was crazy; loud noises followed by silence. Made no sense. He tiptoed toward his office door, pistol out, safety off. He reached for the knob and turned it slowly. He had a full grip on the knob when the door was snatched open, taking him with it. He had time to see Joan sprawled on the office floor before he was struck on the back of the neck with a heavy object. The last thing he heard was a high-pitched laugh from a male.

———

Stone came to slowly, and his hands were secured behind his back. He could see shards of broken glass on the floor in front of him, but he couldn't see anything else.

"Wakey, wakey," a deep voice said. "Damn, Harley, that cane of yours is a magic wand."

"Ain't it?" a higher-pitched voice replied.

Someone sat Stone up and leaned him against a leather club chair. He could see Joan now, sprawled on her back, her .45 a few feet away, cocked. She had fired a round before Harley could shoot at her, he thought. If she had followed his instructions and aimed for the head, somebody must be dead, but who?

"Who's dead?" Stone asked.

"You in just a minute," Wallace said. "All the guests for our party haven't arrived yet. Go upstairs and get her, Harley."

Harley left the room, using a black, metallic cane to make his way.

Wallace Slade picked up Joan's .45, then sat down in the other club chair, facing the door. "Man, it's nice to be in control of things again," he said, chuckling.

Stone watched as Joan began to move, and after a moment, she sat up, looking around her.

"I've got it," Wallace said, showing her the .45.

"You're a lucky guy," Joan replied. "Lucky I don't have it."

"I'd shoot you with your own gun," Wallace said, "but it's too noisy. The neighbors might complain." He held up his silenced 9mm. "This is the right tool," he said. "You always should use the right tool for any job."

"I don't think you want to do that, Wallace," Stone said.

"Why not?" he asked. Then there was a muffled popping noise, and a red splash appeared on his forehead.

"That's why," Stone said.

Jenna came into the room, holding the little silenced CIA pistol ahead of her. "Joan," she said, "I shot him in the head."

"And a very nice job it was, Jenna," Joan replied. "But where's Harley?"

"I shot him in the head, too."

END
November 4, 2021
Washington, Connecticut

AUTHOR'S NOTE

I am happy to hear from readers, but you should know that if you write to me in care of my publisher, three to six months will pass before I receive your letter, and when it finally arrives it will be one among many, and I will not be able to reply.

However, if you have access to the Internet, you may visit my website at www.stuartwoods.com, where there is a button for sending me e-mail. So far, I have been able to reply to all my e-mail, and I will continue to try to do so.

If you send me an e-mail and do not receive a reply, it is probably because you are among an alarming number of people who have entered their e-mail address incorrectly in their mail software. I have many of my replies returned as undeliverable.

Remember: e-mail, reply; snail mail, no reply.

When you e-mail, please do not send attachments, as I never open these. They can take twenty minutes to download, and they often contain viruses.

Please do not place me on your mailing lists for funny stories, prayers, political causes, charitable fund-raising, petitions, or sentimental claptrap. I get enough of that from people I already know. Generally speaking, when I get e-mail addressed to a large number of people, I immediately delete it without reading it.

Please do not send me your ideas for a book, as I have a policy of writing only what I myself invent. If you send me story ideas, I will immediately delete them without reading them. If you have a good idea for a book, write it yourself, but I will not be able to advise you on how to get it published. Buy a copy of **Writer's Market** at any bookstore; that will tell you how.

Anyone with a request concerning events or appearances may e-mail it to me or send it to: Putnam Publicity Department, Penguin Random House LLC, 1745 Broadway, New York, NY 10019.

Those ambitious folk who wish to buy film, dramatic, or television rights to my books should contact Matthew Snyder, Creative Artists Agency, 2000 Avenue of the Stars, Los Angeles, CA 90067.

Those who wish to make offers for rights of a literary nature should contact Anne Sibbald, Janklow & Nesbit, 285 Madison Avenue, 21st Floor, New York, NY 10017. (Note: This is not an invitation for you to send her your manuscript or to solicit her to be your agent.)

If you want to know if I will be signing books in your city, please visit my website, www.stuartwoods.com, where the tour schedule will be published a month or so in advance. If you wish me to do a book signing in your locality, ask your favorite bookseller to contact his Penguin representative or the Putnam publicity department with the request.

If you find typographical or editorial errors in my book and feel an irresistible urge to tell someone, please write to Gabriella Mongelli at Penguin's address above. Do not e-mail your discoveries to me, as I will already have learned about them from others.

A list of my published works appears in the front of this book and on my website. All the novels are still in print in paperback and can be found at or ordered from any bookstore. If you wish to obtain hardcover copies of earlier novels or of the two nonfiction books, a good used-book store or one of the online bookstores can help you find them. Otherwise, you will have to go to a great many garage sales.

ABOUT THE AUTHOR

STUART WOODS is the author of more than ninety novels. He is a native of Georgia and began his writing career in the advertising industry. **Chiefs,** his debut in 1981, won the Edgar Award. An avid sailor and pilot, Woods lives in Key West, Mount Desert Island, and Washington Depot, Connecticut.

STUARTWOODS.COM
FACEBOOK.COM/STUARTWOODSAUTHOR

LIKE WHAT YOU'VE READ?

Try these titles by Stuart Woods,
also available in large print:

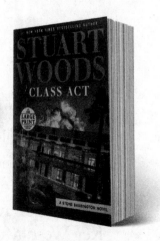

Foul Play
ISBN 978-0-593-45962-1

Criminal Mischief
ISBN 978-0-593-45963-8

Class Act
ISBN 978-0-593-41787-4

For more information on large print titles, visit
www.penguinrandomhouse.com/large-print-format-books